"*C.A. Pack brings a real thriller to life with Becoming Johanna.*"

—*Readers' Favorite Review*

Becoming
Johanna

BOOKS IN THE LOI SERIES

BECOMING JOHANNA
(2016)
Prequel Novella

CHRONICLES: THE LIBRARY OF ILLUMINATION
(2014)
Includes:
The Curator
Doubloons
The Orb
Casanova
Portals

SECOND CHRONICLES OF ILLUMINATION
(2015)
Includes:
Portals
The Overseer
Myrddin's Memoir

THIRD CHRONICLES OF ILLUMINATION
Coming in 2016

Becoming Johanna

C. A. PACK

Artiqua Press

www.artiquapress.com

info@artiquapress.com

Artiqua Press
New York
www.ArtiquaPress.com

BECOMING JOHANNA

ISBN: 09915428-0-0
ISBN-13: 978-0-9915428-0-2

When she was younger,
the prime curator of
The Library of Illumination
wished her life away …

1

PEAKIE'S FOUNDLING HOME was not a pleasant place to grow up. Children—while clothed, fed, and educated—were given little more than the basics, and often found themselves hungry, cold, or abused for not learning their lessons properly. Josefina wished she would grow older quickly and couldn't wait for the day she'd be able to escape the home forever.

She'd been brought to Peakie's when she was three years old. She had hazy memories of a woman, Fina, clutching her, and she anxiously awaited Fina's return. But as the months turned into years, the child finally realized no one would be coming back for her.

When Josefina turned seven, she summoned up the courage to question the matron in charge of her ward. "Why am I here?" Josefina knew there was life outside of Peakie's; wisps of it survived in her memory. The matron waved her away, but the child would not be deterred. Every day she asked the same question. Weeks passed before the matron brought her to see the headmaster. He nodded toward two straight-back chairs in front of his desk, and the matron and child sat down.

"You are asking about your past life. I'm here to tell you it is dead to you. No one is going to come and save you from your chores and schoolwork. There is no idyllic haven that you will be whisked away to in the outside world. You are here until you reach majority, young lady, and I expect you to behave and to stop bothering the matron with questions about your past.

"I will tell you what I know of it now, and there will be no further discussion." He stood up and paced the width of the room. He was a tall, gaunt man with prominent features, and when he stopped walking, he placed both hands on his desk and leaned forward, staring at Josefina with humorless dark eyes. She shivered. "An old man brought you in and said he found you in a dead woman's arms in a library. He told us your grandmother was dead and your parentage was unknown to him. The only thing identifying you was the name embroidered in the hem of the apron you wore—Josefina Charo. We alerted all the proper authorities, but no one claimed you. We searched for relatives, but found none. Your parents are probably dead. Thus, you are here to stay, Josefina. Go back to your classroom and tell your teacher to double your homework to make up for the lesson you missed this morning.

"Let me repeat: No one is coming back for you. Ever."

The matron returned Josefina to the classroom, and the child had a hard time concentrating on her lesson. She usually loved learning new things, but not on this day. Instead, she held her text book up high to shield herself so no one would notice the tears streaming down her face, or the tiny sniffs that punctuated the wretched stillness of the dimly lit room.

Josefina had always been exceptionally bright and had excelled in the curriculum available to her. She quickly surpassed the other students until there were no more classes for her to take. She questioned the matron about continuing her education, but was told flat out that Peakie's Foundling Home would not provide a university education "by any means." Instead, the matron sent Josefina to work in the laundry by day and wait on the younger children during mealtime each night—a tedious existence for a teenage girl overflowing with intelligence and imagination.

Josefina's work schedule prevented her from

participating in outdoor recess. Each day, regardless of weather, students were herded out the door into a side yard surrounded by an eight-foot cement block wall. Half the area was covered in concrete. The other half had a few trees and benches for people who preferred to sit and contemplate life. The sparse crabgrass surrounding the base of the trees had a green tinge, but the rest of the grassy area was brown and would remain that way. Peakie's staff would never spend money on something as trivial as grass seed or fertilizer if they thought children would trample the resulting lawn to death in just a few weeks. So nature took its course, and dozens of feet pummeled the dried up blades of grass, making mowing unnecessary.

During Josefina's long, boring work periods, she planned her escape. Sometimes, when she dragged the trash out to the alley at night, she looked longingly past the gate. It looked dark and forbidding, but she could see lights beyond the alley, and hear threads of conversation and bursts of laughter coming from what lay beyond. All she had to do was climb over the wall.

ONE NIGHT, JOSEFINA witnessed something unusual. A tall boy wearing a hooded sweatshirt ran down the alley, but stopped for a moment to pull money out of a wallet he held in his hand. To Josefina's amazement, he stuffed the money in his pocket and threw the wallet into the gutter, where it nestled among trash that had found a home in its crevices and corners. Josefina's heart beat faster. Her imagination got the best of her. She furtively searched the surrounding area to make sure no one stood watching her and climbed the fence to retrieve the wallet. She had never climbed a fence before and found it daunting. It was not unyielding, and it swayed under her weight. The top had a roll of barbed wire fastened to it, but it looked like others may have taken this route before; the wire was flattened and easier, if just as painful, to climb over.

The wallet was like a small treasure trove. It held no money—the thief had seen to that—but it contained a driver's license, a credit card, and a library card. She scrambled back across the fence. She considered finding the wallet a sign that she should leave. *I have to make plans.* She didn't consider the idea of turning the wallet in. She already knew the matron would throw it out, rather than invite the police into the foundling home. They would probably accuse Josefina of the theft, after all, she had left the grounds, so who's to say she didn't mug the owner? No. This was providence. She had been sent this wallet as a means to an end, the end of her association with Peakie's Foundling home.

She didn't think of the blood the barbed wire left dotting her hands and legs until another girl commented on it.

"I fell," Josefina lied.

"Klutz," the girl replied. "You'd better repair

your skirt before the matron sees it."

Josefina looked down and saw a tear in the fabric. "Right," she muttered. She quickly finished her tasks and rushed to the shower room where she washed off the blood and kitchen stench. That night, after mending her skirt, she lay in bed under the thin blanket allotted to each child and planned her future. The name Joan A. Carr was printed on the driver's license. Initials J. C. just like Josefina Charo. According to the birthdate on the license, the owner was nineteen years old, just a couple of years older than Josefina. *This can't be coincidence. It must be fate.* The library card held an additional morsel of information—Joan *Alice* Carr. Of course, she couldn't become Joan Carr. Someone with that name already lived nearby and was probably in a police station at that moment reporting the theft. No. That name would never do at all. She would have to come up with a way around it. But first, she had to figure out how she would get away.

THE STATE FORCED the foundling home to pay Josefina a meager wage, because she held two positions, exceeding the hours required to satisfy her room and board expense. At first, she carried the money she earned in her pockets and then tucked it in her socks and underwear. When it became too bulky, she slipped it inside the lining of her winter jacket by cutting the stitches on a pocket and then re-sewing it. It wasn't that she had a lot of money, but she was afraid to exchange small bills for larger denominations, because someone who didn't have her best interests at heart—which would be everyone at Peakie's—might try to steal it. No. She would continue to collect her earnings, and when the time was right, she would disappear.

AN ELDERLY MAN with a thatch of wispy, white hair arrived at Peakie's Foundling Home one evening and asked to speak with the headmaster. The girl manning the reception desk relayed the message, but was told the headmaster was too busy for visitors. The man smiled at her when she gave him the answer. "Would you try again? Please tell him Malcolm Trees is here with my annual gift to the home. I wouldn't want to leave with the donation still inside my pocket."

She reluctantly returned to the headmaster's office and cringed when he blasted her for not handling the visitor on her own. "But he says he has a gift—a donation—and he'd hate to go home with it still in his pocket."

That changed everything. The headmaster rushed out with a smile plastered on his face. "Mr. Trees, what a pleasure to see you again."

"As you know, my organization likes to present a small annual endowment to the home for the betterment of the children here."

"Yes, I know, and we fully appreciate it."

"I originally set it up to help defray some of the costs of the little girl I brought you—after she was abandoned in the Library of Illumination. I wonder if I could see the child."

"No ... no. That would be highly irregular. It would never do to single out one child. It causes a disruption among the others—petty jealousies and mean-spiritedness. I couldn't possibly allow it."

"I was really hoping to check in on her, to make sure she's okay." He took a check out of his breast pocket and looked it over. "Of course, if she's not here because she's been adopted, then there's no need." He folded the check and placed it back in his pocket.

"I'm ... I'm sure there wouldn't be any problem if you just look at her from a distance. That way the others won't think she's getting special treatment."

Malcolm Trees relented. "That will have to do."

The headmaster sent the receptionist to ascertain Josefina Charo's whereabouts and inform the matron of their visitor. A short time later, they stood at the entrance to a cafeteria, where lines of children waited to get their dinner.

"The children all look rather young to be the girl I'm inquiring about," the visitor noted.

"That's because she's not in the food line," the matron said. "She's behind the counter, serving peas and potatoes."

The visitor's eyes flashed. "She's hardly old enough to be working here. It looks more like indentured servitude to me."

"It most certainly is not," the matron spit out. "She gets paid."

"Oh," the visitor said, nonplussed. "What about her studies? This can't be helping her."

"She has completed her studies," the matron replied. "She's a sharp one, but not so sharp as to outwit me."

"Has there been trouble?" Malcolm Trees asked.

"No. And there won't be if I have anything to say about it."

"You see," the headmaster broke in, "Josefina is too young to send out on her own, and jobs like this allow her to build up her skills for when she ultimately leaves us."

"If she finished her studies two years early," Malcolm Trees mused, "I can't help but think she's gifted. So you can understand why I'm concerned that you're building her skills as a cafeteria worker rather than getting her advanced tutoring."

The headmaster reddened. "This is just one of the jobs she has here at the home. It's not to teach her how to be a cafeteria worker. It's to teach her responsibility and self-sufficiency."

"Yes, I see," the visitor answered. *I see only too well.*

A FEW WEEKS later, Cook brought Josefina to the market with her. The sights and sounds outside the home were not what the girl expected. Just one block away from the foundling home, a village square bustled with people going about their daily routine. Storefronts captured the girl's attention with their treasures, but she was not allowed to linger and study the displays. Instead, Cook filled the cart Josefina pulled with whatever she needed to stock her kitchen. And when the amount of goods exceeded the room in the cart, she handed Josefina bags to carry as well.

MONTHS PASSED BEFORE Josefina felt she had saved enough money to run away. She'd thought about leaving two months earlier, after she had been sent to the basement to fetch a box of fabric scraps. In the dark confines of the cellar, she discovered a pile of old and broken items destined for the dumpster. A small suitcase—barely twelve by sixteen inches—sat at the top of the heap. It contained no name or identification and now lay abandoned under a thick layer of grime. Josefina hid it in a far corner where it would not be easily discovered and vowed to return for it before she made her get-away.

HER EXCURSIONS WITH Cook taught Josefina just how expensive food and sundry items could be, and she felt she might never save enough money to live on her own. But she knew it was time to leave when the headmaster—complaining about high costs—announced he would be cutting workers' wages.
    This is it.

That night, after all the children had gone to bed, Josefina snuck down to the main office and closed herself inside. She was lucky the lock to the headmaster's door had been broken months before, when he threw a paperweight in a fit of anger, and it shattered against the doorknob, knocking something in the mechanism out of whack. Inside his office, she looked for her name as she went through file drawers aided only by the full moon and a box of kitchen matches. She found the folder and hid it under her clothing.

As she was about to open the door, she heard a floorboard squeak. Someone was outside the office. Her heart thumped. She could hear the blood rushing in her head. She knew if she got caught stealing a file from the headmaster's office, she would be severely punished. Her internal cacophony must certainly be louder than the floorboard in the hallway! She felt sweat bead up on her forehead. She sank down into a low crouch, hoping a large credenza would shield her. She waited for what seemed like an eternity, but no one entered the office. When she finally felt safe, she crept upstairs to the girls' lavatory where she locked herself in a stall to review the folder's contents. It contained correspondence pertaining to her being left at Peakie's, and a record of all her grades and infractions. There was only one offense, and it still hurt to think about the punishment she received for telling the headmaster he was wrong. The last item in the folder was a small card containing a social security number in the name Josefina Charo. She knew she would need the number to make her way in the world and hid the file in her jacket sleeve.

THE FOLLOWING MORNING, Josefina snuck away from the laundry while everyone was busy with work or classes and gathered all her possessions together in a small pile. She didn't have much—a skirt and blouse, a pair of pants and a shirt, socks, underwear, a nightgown, toothbrush, hairbrush, and more importantly, Joan Alice Carr's wallet. Josefina would wear the only pair of jeans she owned with a sweater and her jacket during her *getaway*. She snuck down the back stairs and crammed everything in the suitcase she had found.

The rest of the day dragged on, especially dinner, and she could hardly wait for everyone to go to bed. She waited for their tossing and turning to stop and their breathing to regulate, before she clutched her jacket to her chest and crept down to the basement. She grabbed the suitcase and stealthily made her way toward the back door of the home. CRASH! She jumped when she heard a pot clatter against the kitchen floor followed by a string of expletives. She hid in a shadowy alcove and waited. Whoever had dropped the pot apparently made a mess and took their time cleaning it up. Every minute felt like an hour. Josefina might have fallen asleep if the wild beating of her heart hadn't kept her awake. Finally, she saw Cook's face for an instant, before the woman switched off the kitchen light and groped through the dark to the back staircase.

Josefina tiptoed into the kitchen and felt her feet sticking to the floor. *Smells like oatmeal.* She looked at the empty stove. *Cook dropped the breakfast pot. I guess everyone's getting cold cereal tomorrow. Everyone except me.*

She unlocked the door and eased it open inch-by-inch to keep it from squealing on its hinges and alerting someone to her escape. The beam of a flashlight cut across the rear yard, and she managed to get inside with the door mostly closed just before being caught. She'd heard there was a night watchman but had never actually seen him outside, although she had noticed him once or twice sitting in the lobby by the front door when the weather was nasty.

A few minutes later, she opened the door again. She checked the alley to make sure no one was nearby and moved more furtively. She tossed her suitcase over the fence and threw a towel she had taken from the laundry room over the barbed wire to cushion it. She quickly scaled the fence, glad she had used one of the matron's plush towels as opposed to the ones given to the children—which were practically threadbare—so she only suffered a small cut on her palm. She tried to pull the towel off the barbs, but it stayed snagged. She hated leaving an obvious sign of her escape, but they would figure it out anyway when she didn't show up for laundry duty.

Josefina headed for the lights and laughter at the end of the alley and then stopped suddenly. What if someone recognized her? She thought about it. It would have to be a teacher or student, and they were all snug in their beds because they had to be up early in the morning. Some local merchants might know her face, but they were also probably home at this hour. Anyone who would be out this late was no one she would know, and she proceeded up the alley. She recognized the grocery market from her excursions and knew the bus station was just two blocks away. She walked close to the storefronts, trying to seem inconspicuous.

THE BUS STATION was almost deserted. She approached the window and asked how far twenty dollars would get her on the main line.

"Bellingham."

"Okay."

"How many?"

"How many what?"

"How many tickets do you want?"

"Just one."

"You're not traveling with an adult?"

"My aunt is going to meet me," Josefina lied.

"Does *she* know twenty dollars will get you to Bellingham?"

"I'm calling her, to let her know."

The clerk stamped Josefina's ticket and pushed

it across the counter. She picked it up and started to walk away. "Hey," he called out.

"What?"

"Twenty dollars."

"Oh." She pulled the crumpled bill from the wallet in her pocket and handed it to the man.

He nodded. "Have a good night."

She didn't think she would.

Josefina fell asleep on the bus and failed to get off at Bellingham. She only woke when the driver shook her shoulder and told her they were at the end of the line.

"Where are we?" she asked. "This doesn't look like much of a city."

"It's the bus depot. You fell asleep and forgot to get off at the last stop."

"But what am I going to do here?"

"Not my problem. You're the one who fell asleep."

She sat mute, not knowing what to do.

"See that gate?" He waited for her to nod. "I can let you out through there."

Josefina grabbed her suitcase and walked slowly toward the gate. She had a nagging feeling that she had made a terrible mistake. The only saving grace was a sliver of light sky near the horizon. The sun would be rising soon, and she was far away from the foundling home.

The bus driver unlocked the gate.

"Is there a hotel around here?" she asked.

He studied her. She was no older than his youngest daughter. "None that you have any business staying at." He saw her shoulders slump. "Look, I may know of a place. Let me lock up and I'll take you there."

He led Josefina to his car, and she sat huddled in the passenger seat hugging her suitcase. He drove about a mile before pulling to the curb in an old, neglected neighborhood. "Come with me." He knocked on the door.

The curtains twitched before an elderly woman pulled the door open. "Come for breakfast, have you—" She stopped speaking when she caught sight of Josefina.

"She needs a place to stay."

"How long?" the woman asked. "All the cabins are taken." They both turned to stare at the girl.

"I need to find a place to live," she whispered.

"A rental?"

"Yes," replied Josefina, "a rental."

The woman nodded and pulled a key ring off the wall. "Come on, then." She led Josefina halfway down the block to a small cottage with an overgrown yard. She unlocked the door and flipped the light switch. "It's not much to look at, but it's enough for a little thing like you. This is the kitchen." It was just large enough to hold a tiny sink, a two-burner stove, a mini-refrigerator, and a couple of cupboards. "It's got a window over the sink. That's a very desirable feature."

The next room was twice as long as it was wide; unfortunately, it was only seven feet wide. "This is your combination living and dining room." There were two doors at the end. She ignored one and led Josefina through the other. "And this is your bedroom," the woman said, as if pointing to a suite in a five-star hotel. The tiny room was no bigger than the kitchen. "You'll be impressed to see its got one of those en-suite bathrooms." The bathroom with its rusty shower stall looked dingy but actually appeared to be larger than the bedroom—if only because it also housed a hot water tank and didn't waste space on a bathtub.

"What's behind that door?" the girl asked, pointing to the closed door at the end of the living room.

"I use that for *my* storage," the woman answered. "It's off-limits to you. That's why it's locked."

"Oh," the girl sighed. "I thought it was a closet."

"You can buy one of those cheap wardrobe closets and put it in the bedroom."

Josefina imagined an intricately carved armoire she had seen in an antique store window on one of her few outings from Peakie's. "Okay."

"One month security; one month rent—in advance." Then she told Josefina how much it would cost.

The young girl's face whitened. It would put a huge dent in her savings. Still, it would belong to her. Josefina carefully counted out the bills from her wallet.

"If you're a model renter, I'll let you stay. Next payment is due on the first of the month."

"But this is already the sixth of the month," Josefina said. "I'd be paying for six extra days even though I wasn't here the whole month."

The woman sighed. She took a couple of twenty-dollar bills and shoved them back in Josefina's hand. "Here. You may want to use it for mousetraps."

She followed the woman's gaze and shrieked when she saw a mouse sitting on the stove.

The bus driver grabbed the mouse by the tail and threw him out the door. "That one's gone, but you'd best do what she said. You want to be ready for him when he tries to find his way back in."

The old woman handed Josefina the key and left, taking the bus driver with her. The girl leaned against the wall and slid to the floor. *What have I done?*

Her fear and exhaustion was stronger than her disillusionment, and she fell asleep where she sat.

JOSEFINA OPENED HER eyes and gasped at her surroundings. Then she remembered running away from Peakie's. Sunlight seeped through the bare, filthy windows. She stared at the dingy walls and the dirty floor. She still sat in the same spot she had fallen asleep in earlier that morning. Her stomach growled. *I need food. And cleaning supplies. And something to sleep on.* She left her suitcase in the tiny fridge, hoping it would be safe from mice there. All she had to worry about was the odor of stale milk permeating everything she owned.

She carefully noted her address and memorized how to get back before exploring the area. Her new home was only a few blocks from a shopping area. In the grocery store anchoring one end of the strip mall, she purchased cans of soup and a box of crackers, as well as cleaning supplies. She also bought a cup, a plate, and small pot. The store didn't sell silverware, but she bought a box of plastic utensils to tide her over. She wanted to buy bread and cheese but feared it might be too attractive to mice. Instead, she bought individual cups of noodles that just needed boiling water, and cans of tuna and peas. She spent more on cleaning supplies than she did on food but knew she really needed them.

She walked past all the stores in the strip mall and found a "bargain" store at the opposite end. Inside, she found a futon—a sofa that folded flat into a bed—on sale. "Can you deliver it?" she asked.

"It's going to cost you extra."

"But I'm only a couple of blocks away."

"It's going to cost you extra. Do you want it or not?"

"Okay."

She also selected a card table, a folding chair, a blanket, and a pillow. And an alarm clock. If she was going to get a job, she needed to know the time. She negotiated the delivery price with the salesman, who told her they would deliver her stuff that afternoon. She paid for everything and felt very, *very* poor. She would have to look for a job as soon as possible, but first, she needed to clean her cottage and get settled. An old building sitting opposite the shopping center caught her eye as she headed home. Home. She didn't know whether to laugh or cry but buried the feeling when she realized the timeworn building housed a bookstore. *Artiqua Literaria.* A bell rang when she open the door. Inside, she felt like she had been transported through time. The polished wooden shelves and creaking oak floor, though well kept, looked like they could have been there for a hundred years. She inhaled deeply and recognized the slightest hint of lemon oil.

"May I help you, dear?" A "pink and white" lady sat behind the sales counter. The elderly woman's pale, powdered skin was highlighted by pink cheeks and topped by a cap of frothy white curls.

"Can I look around?"

"Of course, dear. Just be careful. Many of the books are very, very old.

"You can leave your parcels here," she continued. "It will make your visit more enjoyable."

Josefina put down her groceries and walked to the farthest corner to begin her inspection. Each book was more interesting than the one before it. She loved books and had read every one available to her at Peakie's. So much so, the home ran out of books for her to read.

She discovered a first edition of *Heidi* by Johanna Spyri. She was so engrossed in the book, she didn't hear the bell ring when someone else walked in.

The bookstore proprietor greeted her old friend. "Malcolm! I'm so glad you came. I have that manuscript I told you about. You are the only person who could possibly authenticate it." She disappeared into a small office and emerged with a box containing a medieval document written on calfskin vellum.

Malcolm slipped on the pair of cotton gloves he always carried in his pocket and picked up the top sheet. "Intriguing. I won't know until I inspect it against the original, but it would be quite a find if it's real."

"Imagine—a fourteenth century manuscript that contains the missing stories from the original *The Canterbury Tales* by Geoffrey Chaucer. That would certainly put my little store on the map."

"It would, indeed."

"Let me wrap it up for you."

While he waited, Malcolm wandered about. He spied a familiar face, reading. He felt almost certain it was Josefina from Peakie's Foundling Home. *Imagine seeing her so far from the home.* "Excuse me," he said, "but aren't you from Peakie's … "

Before he could finish, the girl shoved the book back on the shelf, grabbed her packages, and fled the store without looking at him.

He removed the hastily replaced book, which stuck out further than the others on the shelf. He took note of it and smiled. *She has good taste.*

JOSEFINA SCRUBBED ALL afternoon and laid out mousetraps where she thought rodents might try to enter. She had just finished washing windows when her furniture arrived.

She had them place the futon on the far end of the living area, and they leaned the folding table and chair in the part of the room nearest the kitchen. They dumped everything else on the futon.

"Thanks." She stood at the door waiting for them to leave. They seemed reluctant to depart until she said, "Don't let me keep you. You must have other deliveries to make."

"Yeah, lady, and we usually get tips when we make them."

Josefina froze. She knew nothing about tipping. She reached into her pocket and pulled out a dollar. "Here."

"You're all heart, lady," the delivery boy said with a sneer. "You'd better keep this. I think you need it more than we do." He stuffed the bill back in her hand and slammed the door as he left.

Josefina felt the sting of tears, but fought it. This is what she wanted—to be on her own—and she'd have to learn the ropes as she went along.

It didn't take her long to set up her new home. She opened the legs to the card table and pushed it into the corner with the chair under it. That took all of ten minutes. She played around with the futon, unfolding the cushion into a bed, and then folding it again into something resembling a couch. That took another ten minutes. She placed her pillow and blanket on top of the cushion, and then put the other items she'd purchased in the kitchen. She boiled some water for tea and ate soup and crackers for dinner. After cleaning up, there was nothing to do, so she put on her nightgown and made up her bed.

She found it hard to fall asleep. Every time a vehicle drove by, the lights illuminated the room. Every distant sound she heard made her think there was a prowler outside. And softer sounds made her wonder if mice were skittering about inside her walls. She'd fallen asleep the night before on the dirty floor quite easily, but tonight—even in her new bed—sleep eluded her for hours.

The next morning, Josefina looked for mouse droppings. She relaxed when she didn't find any. *Okay. I can live here.* Now she needed an income so she could continue living there. She put on her skirt and blouse and walked back to the shopping area, inquiring at every store if they needed help. She struck out there but overhead a woman saying her daughter had just been hired at LOI Book Services. She had no idea what or where that was but figured it couldn't be far. She approached the woman. "Excuse me. I couldn't help hearing that your daughter had just been hired at a book services company. I'm wondering if you could tell me where it's located?"

"You must be a stranger to these parts. It's right in the heart of town, across from the motor vehicle bureau."

"You're right," Josefina admitted. "I am new in town. I just arrived yesterday. Could you point me in the right direction?"

The woman swung her arm in the direction of the grocery store. "It's just down the road a piece—about a mile."

"Thank you," Johanna said, and headed in the direction the woman had pointed. Twenty minutes later, she found herself on the outskirts of the business district. She kept her eyes open for the motor vehicle office. She had an idea that she hoped would work.

Inside the MVB, she found herself waiting in a succession of lines. The woman at the head of the first line told her to stand in a second line, and the man at the front of the second line told her she would have to wait until someone became available to talk to her. She didn't mind the wait at first, but as the hands on the clock slowly made their way around, she became more and more aware of the amount of time being wasted on a wisp of an idea, when she should have been looking for work.

She heard the name Joan Carr announced over the loudspeaker—and froze. What were the chances that a girl whose wallet was stolen near the foundling home would be here today? Then she realized they were calling *her* and walked up to the counter.

"Hi," she said meekly.

"What can I help you with today?" The guy on the other side of the counter was in his early twenties and had a friendly face behind his thick glasses.

"It's my license. I was in such a rush to replace it when it was stolen, I didn't notice that they got the name wrong. It's not 'Joan A.' It's Johanna. And it's not 'Carr.' It's Charette. I just noticed the mistake, and I need a new one in a hurry. I'm going out of town, and I have to take it with me."

"What happened to your picture?"

"I spilled something on it." She didn't go on to say she did it on purpose to make it harder to tell the photo wasn't of her.

The clerk peered at the picture and the information on the card. "How do I know this is your card? Do you have another form of identification?"

She reached for her wallet. She couldn't use the library card or credit card, because they were in the other girl's name. Then her hand brushed against another piece of paper. She pulled it out and stared at the name on the top. She had tried out the name Johanna Charette the day before, when she asked to have her futon delivered. Luckily, they hadn't written the address on her copy. They had scribbled it on a separate form that they taped to the furniture.

"I don't know if this would help," she said, thrusting the yellow receipt into the clerk's hand. She opened her eyes really wide and sighed. "I really need your help."

It took him a while to respond". "And you say everything else is the same?"

"Yes," she answered. "They just muddled the name. Everything was crazy that day," she continued, warming up to her deception. "Something broke down that wasn't supposed to break down, and everyone was running around. I was so interested in watching the chaos that I never checked my license before leaving. Please help me."

Again, he hesitated and looked like he internally debated the veracity of her story. Then, he smiled. "Okay. Give me your information, and I'll have a new one sent out to you."

"No!" she exclaimed. "I mean you can't," she corrected herself. "I'm going out of town, like I said before, and I need it right away."

A real tear slipped down her cheek—a tear of frustration—and the clerk could not bear to hurt a pretty girl during her moment of need. "Okay," he said. "Wait here." He went to one of the many vacant desks clustered behind him and inserted a form. He typed in her information with the corrected name. He returned to the counter with part of the form he had just filled out. "I'm going to have to take another picture. I can't call up your old one right now. And you'll have to take another eye test."

"Okay," she said. She read the eye chart, smiled for the picture, and held her breath while she waited for the machine to spit out the finished product.

"Here you are." He handed her the license. "Is

there anything else I can do for you?"

"No," she whispered, studying the card with her picture and new identity. "This is perfect." She flashed him a smile. "Thank you."

He smiled back. "Any time, *Johanna Charette.* You know where I am if you need me."

She walked out of the motor vehicle bureau and spotted LOI Book Services across the street. She took a deep breath before walking inside. "Hi. My name is Johanna Charette," she said, extending her hand. "I heard you were hiring from a neighbor whose daughter just got a job here. I absolutely love books and spend all my spare time reading. Please tell me you're still hiring."

"What kind of experience do you have?"

Johanna only hesitated a moment. "I have experience working in a school. I think it's so important for children to read."

"You hardly look old enough to have been a teacher."

"I graduated high school early. And," she lied, "I was a student teacher."

"Why did you give up teaching?"

"I moved. And I could really use a job. I'll do anything."

"We have an opening, but you're probably overqualified for it."

"What is it?" Johanna asked.

"We need an account specialist. Someone with excellent telephone and organizing skills who enjoys dealing with the public."

"I'm your girl," Johanna said. She had never had much reason to speak on the phone, but how hard could it be? She could make up for her lack of phone skills with her organizing skills. And she'd be happy to meet the public. *As long as none of them are from Peakie's.*

The receptionist took a form out of her desk drawer and attached it to a clipboard. "Fill this out and return it to me when you're done. Meanwhile, I'll see if there's anyone who can interview you this afternoon."

Johanna wrote her new name and new address on the form. She filled out the other information to the best of her ability. She changed a couple of the digits on the social security number she had taken from Peakie's so she wouldn't be linked to the home. When it came to past experience, she froze. She couldn't write Peakie's Foundling Home as her place of past employment. LOI Book Services might contact them, and Peakie's could try to track her down. Instead, she made up the name of a school in a small town on the other side of the country. Maybe they'd be so impressed by her work skills that they wouldn't care about her lack of experience.

Johanna was right. LOI Book Services needed customer service clerks so badly, they never bothered to check her references. From what she'd told them during her interview, none of her past experience would come into play for this particular job. Besides, it was an entry-level position.

Unfortunately, the position was not what Johanna expected. She thought she would be surrounded by books and interesting people. Instead, she sat at a desk piled high with invoices, and a stack of ever growing book requests. She didn't get to meet the public, just speak with them over the phone, and most customers were gruff, economized their words, and weren't afraid to criticize her when they thought she was wrong. Still, it was better than sweating in a laundry or ladling out what-passed-for-food to youngsters who couldn't differentiate it from the real thing because they had never eaten a wholesome or delicious meal in their lives.

There was a high turnover rate in the office, with new faces coming and going every few weeks. The only exception was Lucinda, a middle-aged woman who would probably die of old age at her desk. Johanna could sense Lucinda marking her territory every time she spoke. To make matters worse, she reminded Johanna of the matron at Peakie's. If ever a relationship was doomed to failure, it was any semblance of friendship between Johanna and Lucinda. But the young girl did manage to cultivate a couple of friendships outside of work.

Johanna ran into Amaranda—a catalogue copywriter—almost every day in the coffee line, and she found Amaranda had a sharp wit and a comical rejoinder for nearly everything said to her. Amaranda had graduated from a college specializing in fashion design and illustration and hoped to work for a major fashion magazine one day. Right now, she only got to write short catalogue descriptions, but she studied all the latest styles and pored over fashion blogs, reading every description and studying the words the writers used.

Then there was the clerk from the motor vehicle bureau. Derrick frequented the same coffee truck and made it a point to say hello to Johanna whenever he saw her. Eventually, he got up the courage to question something she had told him. "Johanna?"

"Yes, Derrick?"

"I thought you had to leave town in a hurry, and that's why you needed your license so quickly."

Amaranda sneezed, jostling Johanna and making her spill the coffee just handed to her. By the time Johanna had recovered, she knew just what to say.

"I was supposed to go away with my father on a trip, but my sister wheedled and whined until he asked me if I would mind staying home while he took *her* on vacation instead. It really made my blood boil, because she always gets what she wants. She's the baby in the family. Anyway, I had given up my job because I thought I'd be spending the summer … away. So, when I heard about an opening here, I decided working in a new place would be my summer adventure. I rented a small cottage across town and settled in."

"Really? You're living here now?"

"Um-hmm. It's tiny, but it's mine."

"Did you change the address on your license?"

"Not yet. I want to make sure I'm going to stay first. My father may have a hissy fit when he finds out I moved away from home."

"Well, you know where to find me when you need to have that done."

"Thanks, Derrick." Johanna smiled to herself. She thought she was going to have to take a bus out of town to another motor vehicle bureau to avoid suspicion when changing her address. But since Derrick offered to do it, she could hardly turn him down.

"Would ... uh ..." Derrick blushed, "would you have dinner with me on Friday?"

She froze. She didn't want to date Derrick but felt she could hardly turn him down. Not to mention, she'd be getting a free meal out of the deal. Still, she didn't want to lead him on, so she lied, something that came all too easily to her lately. "I'd love to have dinner with you, but to be honest, I'm currently dating someone. He's in the military ... in the Middle East."

"Oh." Derrick paused for a second. "I understand, but since I already asked you, I'd still like to take you out ... as a friend."

Johanna smiled. "Okay, Derrick. Dinner would be very nice."

He got his coffee and returned to work with a smile on his face.

"Do you really want to go out with that guy?" Amaranda asked.

"Not on a date, but I certainly don't mind having dinner with him as a friend. I can use all the friends I can get."

"Well then, I hope you enjoy yourself. But next Friday, why don't you go to the movies with me and the girls?"

"Okay," Johanna answered. "It's a deal."

JOHANNA WAS DISAPPOINTED when she didn't receive a paycheck after her first week but thought she had enough savings left to get her to the next payday. Maybe she could even afford a lamp. Sure, she had a futon and a table, but the only lights were in the kitchen and bathroom. She planned to pick up a few books at the library, but she didn't want to read them in the kitchen or the bathroom. After carefully counting her savings, she figured she had enough money for a lamp and maybe even a little table to put it on, as long as she stayed on the lower end of the price range. She stopped by the bargain store on her way home from work and picked out what she wanted.

"You want us to deliver that?"

"No," she said quickly. "I'll take the lamp now and come back tomorrow for the table." She took the money for the purchases out of her wallet.

"We're not in the habit of *storing* purchases. I'm going to have to charge you a fee for that," the salesman said. He reached for the money, but she snatched her hand away.

"On second thought, I'll just take the lamp." She laid half the money on the counter.

The salesman's features hardened. "I can't promise the table you want will be here when you come back for it."

"And I can't promise I won't go to Danny's Den of Deals in town to buy one."

"Really? You're going to carry a table all the way home from town?"

"I will if I have to," Johanna answered. *If it kills me,* she thought to herself.

THAT EVENING AT dinner, Derrick told her all about his dream to study architecture. "My father owns a construction company, and I worked for him during summer vacations, but I want to do more than build someone else's design. He ridiculed my plans to study architecture. He told me contractors, not architects, are responsible for working out the logistics of constructing all the great buildings in the world. According to my father, studying architecture is a waste of time, and I should work with him to build up the company.

"That was the day I stopped working for him. I knew my old man would keep chipping away at my plan to continue my education. So I took a job at the motor vehicle bureau, even though I make less money and it will take longer to save up tuition, because I refuse to abandon my dream to become an architect."

"Following your dream sounds really noble." Derrick reminded Johanna of herself, but she didn't want to talk about her past, so instead, she told him how much the guy at the bargain store had upset her when he tried to wrangle extra money from her.

"You know, if you want me to go with you when you buy the table in town, I can drive it back to your place in my car."

Johanna's mouth dropped open. "You would do that for me?"

Derrick smiled. "That's what friends are for."

"I grew up alone. No one ever helped me out like that before."

A fragment of information poked at his brain cells. His eyes narrowed. "I'm sure your sister would have, if you gave her the chance," he said tentatively.

"I don't have a sister." She suddenly realized she had fabricated a story about her sister going away in her place, to get Derrick to change the name on the license.

"What?"

"At least, that's what I pretend," she continued. "I find her so exasperating that I've written her off completely."

"Oh." Derrick smiled. "For a moment, there, you had me going."

Johanna felt a headache coming on. When she used it as an excuse to ask Derrick to take her home early, it wasn't a lie.

"I'll pick you up tomorrow around one o'clock to go to the furniture store."

"Thanks, Derrick. I'll see you then."

That night, she tried to sleep, but her head pounded, and she had no aspirin. She put it on her virtual list for her post-payday shopping extravaganza.

Johanna had dark circles under her eyes the next day when Derrick picked her up. "You feeling all right?"

"I don't have any aspirin. I just moved in and there are a lot of things I haven't stocked up on yet."

"There's a drugstore down the block from Danny's Den of Deals. We can pick some up. Do you want to go there first?"

"No, I'd better buy the table first. I want to make sure I have enough money."

"I could always lend you money if you need it."

"I can't take your money, Derrick."

"Because your boyfriend wouldn't approve?"

Johanna felt uncomfortable. *That's another whopper I told him.* Creating a new license was one thing; her entire identity had depended on it. But lying to Derrick about having a boyfriend was something else entirely. She did it to spare his feelings. Now she felt trapped in a web of lies. She had never lied before. The punishment for getting caught in a lie at the foundling home had been brutal, and the children there quickly learned to take their chances with the truth, rather than be punished for a lie. Now, everything about her was a lie. She had abandoned her old life only the week before, and apparently, her ideals along with it. She felt her headache returning.

She found an end table at the furniture store that was nicer than the one she had seen at the bargain store—and it cost less—but right next to it stood a small chest made out of beautiful burled wood with three drawers. She had been living out of her suitcase and thought about how nice it would be to actually have drawers to put her clothing in. "How much is this?"

Her face fell when she heard it cost twice as much as the end table.

"Here," Derrick said, handing the salesman a credit card. "I've got it covered."

"I'll pay you back, Derrick, as soon as I get paid. I promise."

"Don't worry about it." He smiled.

But she did worry about it. She gave the salesman all the cash she had on her so Derrick would only have to pay the difference. In the end, she also had to let him buy her aspirin because she had no money left.

He carried the small chest into the cottage and squeezed it in between the couch and the bedroom door. Johanna picked up her lamp from the floor and placed it on the chest.

"Turn it on," Derrick said, "so you get the full

effect."

"I can't," she answered. "I don't have any light bulbs."

He looked around the room at the sparse furnishings. When he had picked her up for their date, she had rushed out the door without inviting him inside. "What's in here?" He walked into the bedroom.

"Nothing."

"And in here?" He looked in the bathroom and saw a single toothbrush sitting in a plastic cup on the edge of the sink and a roll of paper towels.

"It's just a bathroom."

He opened the cabinet under the sink. She had placed her cleaning supplies there, plus an extra roll of toilet tissue.

"How can you live like this?"

"Like what?"

"Without necessities."

"I'm fine."

"Why don't you ask that boyfriend of yours for money?"

"I'm fine," she repeated.

He walked out of the bedroom and straight for the kitchen. He opened the cupboard and saw a single plate, a single cup, and a box of plastic cutlery. Her one pot sat on the stove—empty. He pulled open the fridge. It held what remained of the few groceries she had purchased the first day. "You have nothing."

"I get by."

"Get by? I had to buy you aspirin!"

She wanted to throw the aspirin at him and tell him to get out, but she really needed the aspirin and felt indebted to him. "Derrick, my headache is getting worse. I have to ask you to leave. I'll pay you back on Friday when I get paid." She pushed him out the door and locked it.

She knew she had nothing, but it hurt her pride to have other people remark about it. *I should have gotten the cheaper end table. I could have waited for the chest.* But it was too late. She owed Derrick, and she wondered if he was going to expect interest, in return.

THAT WEEK SHE worked extra hard and didn't even take time for coffee breaks; after all, she couldn't afford to buy coffee. She was so involved in her work she didn't notice the elderly man who came out of her boss's office.

But he noticed her. He inquired about her by name but was told he was wrong—that she was Johanna Charette, not Josefina Charo. *Could the similarity in names be a coincidence? I think not.* He didn't say anything about it to her boss. He would keep her secret.

FINALLY! SHE RECEIVED her first paycheck. Taxes took a bite out of what she expected, but her salary would still go a long way toward helping her become self-sufficient. Except a chunk would have to go to

Derrick for the chest. She had filled it with all her
possessions the day after she got it, with room to
spare. Now she couldn't imagine being without it,
yet she still berated herself for buying it. *I should
have waited until I saved enough money.* She had
enough to pay Derrick, and she could buy food, but
there was little left over for anything else. She had
been rotating the same skirt and pants with two tops
and one sweater she owned for work, but she felt
cheap and frumpy and feared people would make
fun of her. In fact, Amaranda had already pointed
out her lack of clothes sense and threatened to take
her on a shopping spree. It might have been fun, but
now, the cold hard fact of budgeting, and paying
bills, and being on her own, were starting to take
hold.

She dared not buy any more to eat than she
had the previous week, although she did splurge
on a package of small foil wrapped chocolates and
a container of orange juice. She eyed the coffee
longingly but didn't have a coffee pot and still
couldn't afford one if she paid Derrick back. He told
her not to "worry about it." But she did. She didn't
want to be beholden to anyone. But she needed bug
spray and wished she could afford a can of paint so
she could brighten up the dingy walls in her cottage.
The woman who rented it said *she* couldn't afford
to paint it, but if Johanna wanted to, it was all right
with her. She would have to hold off on paint.

She didn't own a phone, or a car, or even a

second pair of shoes. Her jacket wasn't very warm because she had rarely ventured out from Peakie's. And it would be so nice to have another blanket. The nights were getting colder, and the wind whistling through the ill-fitting windows chilled her to the bone. *Oh, and curtains*! She knew she would feel safer, and warmer, and sleep better if she could cover the windows.

After considerable deliberation, she gave Derrick half the money she owed him and told him she'd give him the rest the following week. She used the money she held onto to go on a lunch hour shopping spree with Amaranda and bought a new top, a warm coat, and a pair of boots. Amaranda insisted she buy a scarf as well, saying Johanna could use it with and without the coat to add style. They chatted while they waited on the cashier's line. Amaranda had just started her own fashion blog and asked Johanna if she could use her as a test subject. She took pictures of Johanna's purchases on her cell phone and explained how she could mix and match her clothing for the best effect. When they got to the register, Johanna spotted wristwatches. She had never owned one before and thought how nice it would be to check the time whenever she felt like it. She impulsively grabbed one and put it on the counter with her purchases. The cashier rang it up and announced the total. Johanna pulled out her money and realized she didn't have enough. "I'm a little short of cash." She pointed to the watch. "You can keep that. I can do without it."

"No, you can't," said Amaranda. She handed the cashier her credit card. "I'll pay for this." She turned to Johanna. "You can pay me back next Friday when you get paid."

Johanna hated racking up more debt. *But I really do need a warm coat,* she reasoned to herself. In the end, she capitulated. "Okay."

She was excited about her purchases, and since Amaranda had charged the entire amount, Johanna felt like she had extra cash. She was normally pragmatic, but instead of saving the money, she used it to buy a comforter to keep her warm at night. And curtains. And a coffee pot. And a radio. And real cutlery. And a scented candle.

That evening, Derrick stopped her as she left work to walk home, laden with packages. "I came by to give you a surprise, but it looks like I'd better give you a ride home first. You have way too much to carry." After helping her with her packages, he presented her with a new driver's license. "We can't have you flouting state law by carrying a license with the wrong address on it. I know your family lives at the other address, but it looks like you're slowly setting up an apartment here for a long-term stay. I hope you don't mind that I put the address change through without asking. I wanted to surprise you."

"That's so nice of you." Johanna flung her arms around him and hugged him, then overcome with embarrassment over her sudden compulsion, pushed him away. "Sorry. I got carried away."

"You can get carried away with me any time you like."

"Thanks again," she said. "I wish I could invite you to stay, but I'm ... uh ... having dinner with my landlady."

Johanna leaned against the door after Derrick left and sighed. *Another lie.*

THAT FRIDAY, JOHANNA cashed her paycheck and realized she had barely enough money to pay Amaranda and Derrick and buy groceries. Not to mention, she really needed a toaster and a dress. Derrick had taken her out to dinner a second time, and she felt woefully underdressed at the restaurant he chose. A dress and high heels would be nice. In the end, she put both her friends off another week. There would be plenty of money to pay them as soon as she got settled in.

She spent more than she planned on a really nice dress, a pair of high heels, and a cute little pocketbook to go with them. She also bought a tote bag for work. Her eyes widened when she saw the bill. Once again, she pointed out items the cashier could take off the bill.

"Why do that, honey," the cashier asked, "when I can just open a store account for you, and you'll get ten percent off whatever you buy today?"

Johanna agreed, filled out the credit application,

received a temporary card, and started to carry her packages back home. Then she realized she still had money in her wallet because she had charged everything and took a taxi instead.

That afternoon, she went out again and bought paint, brushes, and a drop cloth, and found out how expensive painting could be. She originally planned to make the walls white, but when the clerk asked "what color white," and she saw all the different variations, she didn't choose white at all. Instead, the store mixed up a pale silvery blue that made her think of ice castles in the sky for the living room, light creamy gold for the kitchen, and a delicate sage green for the bedroom and bathroom. She nearly emptied her wallet to pay the bill, and when she saw them stacking all her purchases on the counter, she realized she'd never be able to lug it all home. She asked the clerk to call a taxi for her, and once again she was broke.

JOHANNA SPENT ALL day Sunday painting her tiny cottage. She felt a new sense of place—of home—when she applied her last brush stroke. She discarded the supplies and plastic drop cloths that littered the floor and furniture, then threw open the windows and sat on her futon wrapped in her new blanket—in the cold—while she waited for the paint to dry and the odor to dissipate. As she sat there, she envisioned what the space would look like with curtains, a picture on the wall, and an armoire in the bedroom for her clothes. The dress she had just purchased remained in a thin plastic garment bag hanging from a nail sticking out of the bathroom door.

She thought of her finances. She owed money to Derrick, Amaranda, and the department store. To make matters worse, her rent was due the following week. Her stomach flip-flopped when she realized she couldn't pay them all. She would have to put her friends off again. Her rent was going to eat up her entire paycheck. At least the department store hadn't sent her a bill yet. She hoped it would forget all about her but knew it was only a matter of time.

The next day, her boss told her he needed her to work on a special weekend project. "It's important. I need you to stay late Friday to start the inventory and come in Saturday and Sunday until it's done. Everyone else has commitments. You're the only one who can do this. Your job depends on it."

"Will there be additional pay for it?"

"We'll work something out."

In a way, Johanna was relieved. It meant she had an excuse not to see Derrick or Amaranda, and perhaps by the time she did, she might have the money to pay them.

IN THE DAYS that followed, Johanna found herself avoiding both her friends. For the first time, she felt happy about not having a phone. It meant neither of them could easily reach her.

After work on Friday, her manager brought

her back to the warehouse. She had never been there before and was overwhelmed by its sheer size. "What do I have to do?" she asked.

"Count the books. All of them."

"Who will be helping me?"

"It's just you. No one else is available. We need this as soon as possible so our accountant can submit it with our year-end assets summary." He handed her a clipboard filled with blank forms. "If you need more forms, there's a copy machine up there." He pointed to a door connected to the main floor by a rickety set of stairs. "I'd better unlock it for you."

He soon returned and handed Johanna a couple of extra pencils. "Use a new form for each shelf, and be sure to write the shelf number on top." He showed her where to find that information. "Normally, we would ask you to write down the ISBN for each carton of books." Johanna felt faint. "But seeing that you're doing this alone, we'll make do with just the total number of cartons on each shelf. That is, unless the box is open. Then we'll need you to count the books inside and give us an item count." He pointed to a tall metal ladder on a runner. Every bank of shelves had one. "You can use that to inspect the boxes on the top shelves. Make sure they're not open. If they are, we'll need an item count. And that's it. Have a nice weekend!"

Johanna felt overwhelmed but knew the only way to get past it would be to begin. *Start at the top*, she told herself, *while I still have strength.*

She shivered as she started counting cartons. The wind howled outside, and it didn't feel like there was any heat inside the warehouse. Hours passed. She hadn't eaten since lunchtime, when she had consumed a peanut butter and jelly sandwich that she brought from home. It was closing in on midnight, and she was cold, tired, and hungry. She looked at the sections she had finished. Maybe, if she were lucky, she was ten percent done. She'd have to work faster if she wanted to get done on time. But right now, she needed sleep. She walked to the door and tried to pull it open. It was locked. She looked around for a key but couldn't find one. Not hanging on a nail nearby; not in the desk in the office; nowhere. She was stuck there. *I can die here and no one will miss me until Monday.* She carried her coat and bag up to the tiny office and closed the door. It wasn't much warmer, but at least she couldn't hear the wind whistling quite as much. She sat at the desk and put her head down and immediately fell asleep.

She woke up with a blazing headache and a crick in her neck the following morning. Then, her stomach rumbled. She looked through the desk again for something that had caught her eye the night before. She found it tucked between a box of staples and a container of paper clips—a granola bar. She took it and got herself a cup of water from the water cooler. She nibbled the bar and took sips of water, praying it would fill her up enough to keep her going until someone let her out. After her impromptu breakfast, she returned to counting. It was mindless work and she allowed her thoughts to wander back to the foundling home. She had been miserable there, but at least it was hot in the laundry. Too hot, perhaps, but she would welcome that steam right now. Then she thought about the cafeteria. The food was like pigswill, but at least it filled her stomach three times a day and she didn't have to worry about where her next meal would be coming from. *I should have stayed longer. Saved a little longer. I wouldn't be stuck in here right now, if I had.*

That evening, she guesstimated she was halfway done with the inventory. Though exhausted, she rummaged through the rest of the warehouse to see if there was any more food. She found a bag of licorice in a metal desk in the receiving area, as well as a can of soda. *A veritable feast.* She ate half the candy and drank the can of soda. Then she managed to count a couple more shelves before exhaustion set in.

On Sunday, she pushed herself to finish the job. She worked straight through until the last book was counted. By then it was ten p.m. She knew that because she owned a watch that had put her into hock. She wondered how much the company would pay her? She had been there all weekend. If she didn't get out until Monday morning, she would have spent sixty hours straight in the warehouse. That was like a week and a half's pay. More if they paid her overtime. *They have to pay me overtime.*

That would help straighten her bills out.

She woke up Monday morning when she heard the bay door open. She looked at her watch. Six a.m. She picked herself up and straightened her clothing. She slowly descended the stairs. The lack of food made her lightheaded.

"Hey, you," the foreman called out. "What are you doing in here?"

She explained why she was there. The foreman's eyes widened when he heard she was locked in all weekend without food. He handed her a brown bag with his lunch in it. "It's just a couple of bologna sandwiches and an apple, but you're welcome to it."

Johanna really wanted to go home and shower, but she was too hungry to refuse. "Just one sandwich please, and I'll be on my way."

A second warehouse worker walked in. "Hey, who's your friend?"

"She was told to do the inventory—by herself—and they locked her in." Johanna would have added to the story, but she was too busy eating. "So I gave her my lunch. She looks a little shaky. Maybe you ought to drop her at home."

"Do you live far?" the worker asked.

She gave him her address, and he gave her a lift to her cottage. She showered and changed, but dared not lie down—even for ten minutes—or she might fall asleep and be late for work. Instead, she walked back to town to start another week.

JOHANNA LIVED ON instant soup and peanut butter sandwiches all week, and avoided going out the front door at work because she didn't want to run into Amaranda or Derrick until she had their money.

Finally, it was payday. She ripped open her pay envelope and stared at the check. *No!* She marched inside her boss's office and waved it in his face while she repeated how she had been locked in the warehouse for sixty hours and deserved time and a half for that, besides her regular salary, but the check was made out for one week's pay, the same amount she received every week.

"Now, Johanna, don't get upset. I'm just waiting for the higher ups to approve the time sheet you submitted. They're having a hard time understanding how you could put in for one hundred and three hours of work for a single week. They weren't going to pay you at all, until I convinced them to at least let me pay you for your regular work week. We'll sort it out."

She left his office with tears in her eyes, snuck out the back door, and walked home. As she turned the corner in front of her landlady's house, she spotted Derrick's car parked in front of her cottage. She didn't make it that far.

"Johanna, I have to talk with you about the rent."

She turned to see her landlady standing in the doorway. "I paid the rent. In cash. It couldn't have bounced."

"No, dear. It's just that a realtor was nosing around here, inquiring about the cottages. Apparently, some big mucky-muck is thinking of buying them all. So I brought an appraiser through your cottage to see what it's worth. I explained I had a tenant, and he asked what I was charging you, and when I told him, he said the place looked so fresh and clean, I could probably get twice as much."

"Fresh and clean? I'm the one who made it fresh and clean. I'm the one who painted the inside. And washed the windows. And pruned the overgrown bushes in the front yard."

"You did use my shears to do that. Besides, you don't have a lease, dear. I don't believe you have anything spelling out how much the rent would be on the cottage. I'm asking you to sign a lease now. I don't want to double your rent, dear, but I do have to raise it a couple of hundred dollars a month. It's only fair."

"But I'm the one who paid to fix it up," Johanna argued.

"It was a diamond in the rough. The value was always there. You got off cheap for a while. It's best that you sign this lease, or I can't promise the rent won't go up again."

"Are you going to pay me for the paint and cleaning supplies I used to get it so clean?"

"We already discussed that. I told you I couldn't afford it but graciously allowed you to do it if you were willing to bear the expense."

Johanna signed, reluctantly. "Can I use your bathroom?"

"Your own bathroom is just a few doors away. Don't tell me you can't make it that far?"

"I can't. Please?"

"Okay, go ahead, but don't touch anything. I don't go in for snoops, and I'll know if you move anything or open the medicine cabinet."

Johanna knew she couldn't hide out in her landlady's bathroom. She just hoped Derrick would give up and go away. When she walked back in the living room, she saw her landlady staring out the window.

"Are you trying to avoid those two people parked in front of your cottage?"

"Two people?"

"Yes. A young man, whom I've seen entering your apartment with you on occasion. And a dark complexioned girl with flaming red hair."

"Amaranda."

"Why are you avoiding them?"

"I owe them money. I fully intended to pay them back today, but I don't make that much money and you just raised my rent. I was supposed to get paid for working all last weekend on a special project for work, but they haven't paid me yet, so I don't have their money. I feel too ashamed to see them right now."

"Well, you can't stay here, so you're just going to have to see them, aren't you?"

"Yes, ma'am."

Johanna walked out of her landlady's house, ready to face the music. She was just in time to see Derrick and Amaranda pull away. *Thank God.* But she knew they'd be back, and unless she wanted to hide in the dark all weekend, she'd have to apologize and beg their forgiveness.

DERRICK AND AMARANDA didn't return, and Johanna felt optimistic when she went to work on Monday, hoping to straighten out the pay snafu with her boss.

"I have a check for the special project you worked on." He handed her a check for three hundred dollars.

"No. This is wrong. I worked overtime. Plus, I was locked in. I should get time and a half for the extra sixty-three hours I worked here."

"I've been informed that special projects are reimbursed separately from regular hours worked. This project was budgeted as a two-day job at one hundred fifty dollars a day. It's contract labor. We gave you the full amount. You'll have to pay the taxes on your own."

"No. This can't be."

"It can be, and it is. That is all, Johanna. You may leave now." He shooed her away with a flick of his wrist.

Johanna felt her face flush with anger, but she refrained from arguing with her boss. It would only waste time, and he would probably dock her regular pay. Instead, she tried to think ahead. At lunchtime, she would cash the check and give the cash to Derrick, to settle her debt with him. After work, she would return the dress, bag, and shoes she'd purchased and pay back Amaranda. And that would be that.

The rest of the morning dragged, probably because she was anxious to get on with her life. At the stroke of noon, she popped out of her seat.

"Hold on, Johanna. You're not going anywhere." Lucinda, who rarely uttered a word to her, was staring at her intently. "I have to leave early today and was told to give you the invoices I've been working on. You can't leave until I give them to you with explicit instructions. And I can't give them to you until I'm done with them."

Johanna sat down and waited. She watched the long hand on the clock slowly make its way to the quarter hour, and then to half-past, before Lucinda finally handed her a large pile of paperwork. "All of these have to be double-checked for accuracy, and then each customer has to be called with the price and must agree to it in advance of shipment."

Johanna stared at the invoices. "This will take more than one afternoon."

"That's your problem," Lucinda said as she grabbed her bag and raced toward the door. She turned before exiting. "And you'd better get them done," she said with a scowl before finally leaving.

Johanna gritted her teeth as she headed to the

bank to cash her check. She had already wasted a half-hour of precious time waiting for Lucinda. She would be lucky if she had any time left to eat.

She cashed the check and concentrated so intently on counting the money in her hand, she didn't see a car pulling away from the curb. The driver hit Johanna. The crisp twenty dollars bills she'd clutched in her hand moments before shot into the air, and the wind scattered them about. Johanna couldn't have chased them down even if she wanted to. The impact had knocked her down and broken her leg. The car sped off. A small crowd gathered around her. One person called for an ambulance, while another ran for a police officer.

As the ambulance crew lifted Johanna into the back of the vehicle, a woman approached them and handed Johanna three twenty-dollars bills that she and her children had retrieved.

"But this is only sixty dollars … "

"The rest got away," the woman answered. "Either the wind carried your money off, or passing opportunists did."

Johanna didn't know what to say. She felt her lower lip quivering.

An onlooker admonished her. "You could say 'thank you.' She didn't have to give the money back to you. No one else did."

"Thank you," the injured girl whispered.

AN EMERGENCY MEDICAL technician wheeled Johanna

into the busy hospital on a gurney. Every seat in the waiting room was taken. Wheel chairs and gurneys occupied with waiting patients lined the walls. A worker grilled Johanna with personal questions and asked for her insurance card. Johanna explained that she had none and was given another form to sign—stating she would be responsible for paying back the cost of medical treatment. She felt overwhelmed. Her head began to swim and she fainted. A while later, she felt a nurse tapping on her face and saying her name over and over. The odor of spirits of ammonia made her gag.

"Where am I?" Johanna asked.

"You're still in the ER. We can't start treatment until you finish filling out these forms." The woman shoved a pen in Johanna's hand and held a clipboard up to her face. "Sign here," she said, pointing to the appropriate line, "and here."

Johanna scribbled her name and closed her eyes, wishing more than ever that she had never run away from the orphanage.

Doctors fitted a cast to support Johanna's broken leg, and she was given a pair of crutches and a small container of painkillers. The staff seemed reluctant to let her go without the help of family, but after Johanna told them for what seemed like the one-thousandth time that she had just moved to the neighborhood and had no family, they agreed to put her in a taxicab.

The good news was the hospital would bill her.

The bad news was she didn't think to write down the license plate of the car that hit her. Still, the police might have it. She would have to track it down, when she could.

Her immediate problem would be getting to work. She couldn't afford to take cabs every day, and she couldn't ask Derrick or Amaranda to help when she owed them both money. She thought about losing the money she had planned to use to pay Derrick—and cried. *Life shouldn't be this hard.*

Someone banged on her cottage door. She hobbled over and pulled it open, even though she was in no mood for company. She found Derrick and Amaranda standing there.

"You know … " Amaranda began, before her eyes widened. "What happened to you?"

"I went to the bank to cash a check so I could pay you and Derrick back, and I got hit by a car. I'd just come out of the bank and was holding the cash in my hand and it went flying. Most of the money flew off or was pocketed by people on the street. Now I've lost a half-day of work. My leg is broken. And I have no insurance. So just say what you want to say and get it over with, because I know I'm a terrible friend, and I deserve whatever you spit out at me." By this time, she had staggered back to the futon and sank down. Her stomach growled—memorably.

"When was the last time you ate?" Derrick walked over to the refrigerator and opened the door. He found a half loaf of bread, peanut butter, jelly, and an open box of instant soup. "I can't believe you still have no *real* food."

"I've had other things to worry about," Johanna answered.

Amaranda sat next to her on the futon. "Are you going to sue?"

"No. Who would I sue?"

"The guy who hit you with his car."

"How do you know it was a guy?"

"Because I saw the accident. I just didn't know it was you. I was too busy running after … hmmm … I guess you can deduct twenty dollars from what you owe me. I grabbed it off the sidewalk. I would have grabbed more, but some juvenile delinquent—who should have been in school, I might add—beat me to the other bills."

Johanna sighed but didn't speak.

"I'm running down to the sandwich shop in the strip mall. What do you want?" Derrick asked.

"I'll take a BLT and a diet soda," Amaranda answered.

"Nothing for me," Johanna mumbled, closing her eyes.

"Wrong answer. It's my get well gift to you—a sandwich and a soda. What will it be?"

"It doesn't matter."

"Okay. Then I'll decide for you." Derrick walked out the door with his keys in his hand.

"Does it hurt?"

Johanna opened her eyes. "Only when I

breathe."

"Did they give you any painkillers?"

"I guess that's what they are. Look in my coat pocket." Her coat lay in a heap on the floor where she had shrugged out of it.

Amaranda picked it up and removed a pill bottle from the pocket. "This is pretty heavy duty stuff."

"I'm sure I wouldn't know."

"You'd better wait till Derrick gets back and eat first. Then take one of these and we'll leave you so you can get a good night's sleep."

"I hope it works. I need to get up early, because I think it's probably going to take me twice as long to walk to work."

"Walk to work! Are you crazy? You need to rest a couple of days. And even then, you can't walk there. It's too much, too soon."

"I have to go. I don't get sick days, and if I don't work, I don't get paid. Not to mention, I could lose my job." An image of Lucinda's angry face popped into her mind.

"It doesn't sound like much of a loss, if you ask me."

Johanna clammed up. She knew Amaranda would counter everything she said. It would be better not to argue and just to let her friend think she had won this round. The next thing she knew, Derrick woke her up to eat.

"I wasn't sure what you'd like," he said, "so I

got you a turkey and cheese hero, and a BLT like I got Amaranda, and a chicken salad sandwich in case you didn't want either of the other two."

Amaranda dragged over the folding table and chair. She unwrapped her sandwich and took a bite. "Love ... B ... L ... Ts," she said between chews.

"Which sandwich do you want?" Derrick asked Johanna.

"Take whichever one you want."

"I've got rare roast beef on rye with Russian dressing."

She wrinkled her nose. "I'll take the chicken salad, I guess."

He unwrapped it for her and opened a can of soda. Then he sat down and dug into his own food.

Amaranda stopped eating and held up her hand. "I'll bet this is your first dinner party."

Johanna gave her a crooked smile. "It's more like Derrick's dinner party."

"He's just the caterer. It's your home, so it's your dinner party."

Derrick pulled out his cell phone and took a picture. " For the society pages ... "

Johanna took a pain killer for dessert, while Derrick put the extra sandwiches and soda in her fridge.

"It's there when you get hungry." He kissed her forehead.

Amaranda gave her a hug. "We'll come by after work tomorrow. And don't get any ideas about walking there in the morning. You've got to stay home with your leg elevated so the swelling goes down. If you do that, it won't hurt as much, and you won't need painkillers, and then you'll be able to return to work. But. Not. Tomorrow."

"My boss. I have no phone."

"I'll pop in and tell him," Amaranda said as she pulled the door closed.

THE NEXT MORNING, Johanna slept through the alarm. She dragged herself into the kitchen, and made a pot of coffee. She was going to make a peanut butter sandwich until she saw the sandwiches Derrick had left behind. She ate half the turkey hero instead, and it felt good to have a full stomach.

Her leg began to throb and she took another painkiller. She sat on the futon with her leg on the folding chair and alternated between reading and dozing off all day. At five o'clock, she pulled herself together so she'd look presentable when Derrick and Amaranda arrived.

A short time later, the three of them shared a pizza while Amaranda recounted her conversation with Johanna's boss about her broken leg. "He's such a jerk. He went on and on about how you're not entitled to sick days and said he'd almost asked management to fire you when you 'failed to' return to work yesterday afternoon. He seemed to know all about the accident, just not that you were the victim."

"Really, Johanna," Derrick said between

chews, "you should look for a job somewhere else, where they treat their employees with respect."

Amaranda laughed. "Does such a place even exist?"

"Don't worry about it. I'm feeling much better," Johanna lied. "I guess I'll face his wrath tomorrow."

Amaranda shook her head. "Absolutely not. I know you don't get paid for staying home and all, but you really need to take one more day."

"I'm bored," Johanna replied. "I might as well be bored at work. I can sit with my leg up there just as well as I can do it here. I owe both of you money and my landlady just raised my rent."

"Okay," Derrick broke in, "but don't walk. I'll pick you up in the morning."

"Thanks. I don't know how I'll ever repay you."

"Oh, I can think of a few ways."

Johanna felt her stomach lurch. She liked Derrick as a friend. Nothing more.

Amaranda sighed deeply.

Johanna fidgeted. "You're upset that I'm returning to work?"

"Christmas is next week. I'm upset because I'd hoped you would pay me back before then. Now I see it's impossible."

"I'm sorry. I had Derrick's money in my hand when the car struck me, and I was going to run to the store after work and return the dress and shoes I bought, so I could pay you back."

"You bought a dress? Without me? Where is it?"

"Hanging in the bag on the bathroom door."

Amaranda slipped away, leaving Johanna alone with Derrick.

"Don't worry about paying me back," he said. "Consider it a combination house warming and get well gift."

"I do worry, and I *will* pay you back. We're friends, Derrick. And friends don't take advantage of friends." She hoped he got the message.

Amaranda walked in and modeled the dress. "How do I look? You don't have a full length mirror, so I can't tell."

"Nice!" Derrick said appreciatively.

Johanna's eyes opened wide. "It looks spectacular on you."

"The holiday party where I work is this Friday. Would you consider lending it to me?"

How can I say no? "Sure."

"The shoes are a little tight," Amaranda continued, "but they go so well with the dress, I don't mind suffering a little."

Johanna shrugged. Amaranda was bigger than Johanna and had more curves, so she undoubtedly weighed more. By the time she returned the dress and shoes, they would no longer be pristine and would probably be stretched out. Then a little light bulb went off in Johanna's head.

"That dress and those shoes add up to almost

what I owe you. I also bought a small purse that will actually make the outfit worth more than that. Would you be willing to take the entire *ensemble* as payment for my debt?"

"Where's the purse?"

"Open the top drawer of the chest. It should still be in the bag."

Amaranda ripped open the bag like a kid at Christmas. "Ohhh. This is perfect." She turned to Derrick. "You're sure it looks all right?"

"You look like a million bucks," he said.

Amaranda gave Johanna a dazzling smile. "It's a deal!"

THE NEXT MORNING, Derrick knocked on Johanna's door right on time. He helped her navigate the two steps down to the sidewalk and held her crutches while she got into the car. They made small talk until they got to LOI Book Services. "Will you be able to get inside by yourself? I thought it would be better to drop you off here before I park the car."

"I'm fine, Derrick. Thanks."

"I'll pick you up here at five-oh-five, unless you want me to bring you lunch?"

"You already did."

"Huh?"

She took a half turkey hero out of her bag. "I'm still stocked with food you brought over the other night. I'll see you at five. Five-*oh*-five." She shuffled to the front door and someone held it open for her as she disappeared inside.

Johanna found her desk PILED with work—not only her regular work, but also the pile of invoices Lucinda had foisted upon her a few days before. She sat, turned her empty trashcan upside down, and hoisted her broken leg on top to keep it elevated. It throbbed because she refused to take a painkiller before going to work. She started entering invoices and didn't look up until she heard people leaving for lunch. That's when she realized everyone, except her, had gone out. Not one person asked if they could bring anything back for her. *They* didn't know she brought lunch from home. She felt the sting of tears and tried to blink them away. She felt totally isolated. *The least they could have done was ask.*

The clock struck one, but the room remained empty. Johanna didn't let her curiosity stop her from working. By the time the other employees trickled back in, she had finished her paperwork and started returning the phone calls that had come in over the past day and a half. Her co-workers seemed to be in a good mood, even if the clients who had been waiting for their return calls did not.

"Where did everyone go?" she asked Lucinda.

"Office holiday party."

"Oh," Johanna gasped. "I forgot all about it."

"You weren't missed," Lucinda answered, pulling a lint ball off the sleeve of her sweater and flicking it away.

Johanna felt like she had been slapped in the

face. She tried to be nice to everyone, but after working there more than a month, she still felt like an outsider.

A guy, who sat a few desks away, placed some snowflake cookies wrapped in a paper napkin on her desk. "I saw you couldn't get out to the party, so I brought a little of the party back to you."

She felt a flush of emotion. "Thank you," she said. His small act of kindness contrasted sharply with Lucinda's nasty retort.

By the end of the day, Johanna had caught up on her work. Just two more days and LOI Book Services would close shop for the four-day holiday weekend. She wouldn't get paid for Christmas Eve or Christmas Day, but she wouldn't lose her job either. Everyone had to take those two days off— whether they wanted to or not.

AFTER GOING TO the bank to cash their paychecks, Derrick dropped Johanna off at her door Friday evening. "See you next Thursday. I'll pick you up for work in the morning."

She did a double take. "Not until Thursday?"

"It's Christmas. If I don't fly home and spend time with my family, my mother will hunt me down and kill me. Or nag me to death. And she'll never let me leave on Christmas Day. I have very little choice in the matter."

"Oh, right. I don't know what I was thinking." She handed him the money she owed him.

"I told you it was a gift."

"It's too generous a gift," she said. "And it doesn't include all the meals you've bought me, or the rides you've given me. Please take it."

INSIDE, JOHANNA COLLAPSED on the futon. Derrick was going home for the holidays. Amaranda had wished her a Merry Christmas before leaving the previous night with her new dress and accessories. She'd announced she was going on a family ski trip and wouldn't be back until after the New Year. Johanna hadn't anticipated being all alone for the holidays. She thought about Peakie's. She'd hated it there, but at least other people were always around. The previous year, the staff had organized a Christmas Eve concert featuring a chorus of some of the children. The next day they'd served a turkey dinner. *She* served the turkey dinner. Cook specifically told her each child could only have one slice of turkey, and she'd better not see Josefina dishing out any more than that. Johanna tried to make it look like more by placing it on top of the brussel sprouts everyone hated, and pushing it close to the dressing, then dumping gravy on top. By the time she got to eat her own dinner, it was cold. It didn't seem like much of a meal then, but it was better, in comparison, to the peanut butter and jelly sandwich she would probably eat alone on Christmas Day.

BOREDOM OVERCAME HER the next day. She could have

worked on the cottage if she didn't have a broken leg. She finished reading the books she'd borrowed from the library and craved more, if only to occupy her mind. She could take a cab to the library but hated wasting what little money she had left. She decided, instead, to walk there. It wasn't as far as the town center, although it was easily a mile away. It should have been a pleasant walk on a sunny, cloudless day; however, unusually cold temperatures and the fact Johanna's leg throbbed made it a grueling journey. By the time she reached the library, she begged them to allow her to put her foot up on a chair to help alleviate the swelling.

"You must want a particular book very badly to walk here on crutches on such a cold day."

"No," Johanna replied. "I just ran out of books to read and I wanted a few new ones."

"Well, now, let me see what we have," the librarian said, embarking on a search for new releases.

A half hour later, Johanna made her choices.

"How will you get these home?" the librarian asked.

"The same way I brought the returns with me. I'll put them in a plastic bag and tie the bag to the handle of one of my crutches."

"Doesn't that throw you off balance?"

"It hasn't yet." Johanna watched a woman walk out of a nearby office carrying a plate of food and a glass of punch. The woman placed it on a desk and took her place behind it.

The librarian noticed. "It's our holiday party," she explained. "Can I get you some punch or a cup of mulled apple cider? Have you eaten yet? I could make you a plate of food. We have more than we can possibly eat."

Johanna wanted to say "no, thank you," but her stomach chose that moment to growl, and the word, "Okay," slipped out when she opened her mouth.

"You wait right here." The librarian disappeared into the office and re-emerged a few minutes later with food and cider.

Johanna thanked her and dug in. She found life to be either "feast or famine," and she knew she should feast before famine inevitably returned.

"Do you have plans for the holidays?" the librarian asked, making conversation.

"Thanks to you, I plan on curling up with a good book."

"No big holiday dinner plans?"

"No … but this," Johanna pointed to the plate of food the librarian had given her, "more than makes up for it."

A woman and her daughter rang the bell on the circulation date. "I'd better get that," the librarian said, turning.

Johanna nodded as the librarian rushed away. "Thank you," she called out.

Ten minutes later, Johanna hobbled home with a bag of books tied to her crutch and a belly filled with food.

BY CHRISTMAS EVE, Johanna had finished reading all her library books and boredom returned. She felt cooped up and isolated and a little depressed that she had no one to celebrate the holidays with. She consoled herself with the fact that she wouldn't have to spend extra money that she didn't really have on gifts and decorations.

If the weather had been unseasonably cold just before Christmas, it turned unusually mild for Christmas Eve. It beckoned her outside, and she grabbed her crutches and slowly made her way up to the strip mall. At the corner, she rested by a temporary Christmas tree lot. It wasn't as crowded as she thought it would be on Christmas Eve, and she said as much to the young man selling trees.

"Everyone who wants a tree, pretty much has one by now. I'm here for the holdouts—you know— the parents who want their kids to think Santa put up the tree. They're the Type-A variety who drink designer coffee and run on adrenaline and nicotine."

Johanna pointed to a scrawny tree that was barely two-and-a-half feet tall. "What will happen to trees like that one?"

"We'll feed it to the chipper and sell the mulch in the spring."

"Oh." She didn't mean for it to sound like a gasp, but she felt sad about the tiny tree's fate.

"Where'd you get your tree?" he asked.

"I don't have one."

"I'm guessing you couldn't wrestle one home with that broken leg."

"No. At least not a big one." She looked at the little tree longingly. "How much is that one?" As soon as she said it, she wished she hadn't. She could see her landlady with her hand out for the rent and hear Derrick's veiled suggestions about how she could repay him in lieu of cash. She couldn't afford to splurge money on a dead bush.

He looked her over. She was kind of cute, even on crutches. "No one should go treeless at Christmas, and that little guy won't make much mulch, so if you want him, you can have him. Free. But how are you going to get him home? I'd help you, but I have to stay here for last minute buyers."

Johanna's face brightened. "Maybe you could tie it to my crutch."

"I could do that." And so he did, and Johanna limped home with a smile on her face because *she* would have a tree for Christmas.

"Merry Christmas," he called out as she limped away.

"Merry Christmas," she replied.

As JOHANNA TURNED the corner to her cottage, she saw a delivery truck pull away from the curb. On her top step lay a package wrapped in brown paper. She slowly climbed the two steps to her door, being careful not to knock off any tree needles. She'd lost a few during her trek home, and she didn't want to sacrifice any more. The tricky part would be picking up the parcel. But saving the tree was more important to her. She slipped her key in the lock and went inside but left the door open to make sure no one swiped her package.

She grabbed a knife from the kitchen drawer, so she could cut the string binding the tree to her crutch, and placed the little tree on her table. Returning to the front door, she leaned her crutches against the wall and held onto the doorjamb while she slid down far enough to reach the package. Lifting it turned out to be harder than she thought. She couldn't bend the leg with the cast, so she had to slide it outside the door and along the step. There was no way she could pick up the package with one hand and lost her balance, ending up on her butt. That was fortuitous, because she now had two hands free to grab the package and pull it inside. The trick would be finding a way to get up again from the floor. In the end, she left the package on the floor and wiggled across the living room so she could hoist herself up on the sofa. At least she'd managed to kick the door shut with her good leg on her way to the futon, but in doing so, she'd knocked over her crutches, which now lay on top of the package. Her little adventure and perplexing problem exhausted her, and before retrieving them, she closed her eyes to rest and quickly fell asleep.

THE SUN HAD set by the time Johanna awoke, and she switched on the lamp to look at her watch. It was ten p.m. She caught site of her little tree and smiled. She used the folding chair like a walker and pushed it toward her crutches. A sense of empowerment washed over her as she sat on the chair, leaned down, and retrieved the fallen crutches. With that problem out of the way, she grabbed a magazine Amaranda had given her and made a paper chain out of strips of the more colorful illustrations. She twisted each strip and then wet the ends and twisted them together. Her first attempt looked large and cumbersome, but time was on her side, and she used it to make a finer chain with smaller loops to suit her tree's proportions.

She quieted her growling stomach with a peanut butter sandwich. The bag of chocolates she had purchased as an occasional treat sat in the fridge next to the bread. Each piece had been wrapped in either red or green foil for the holidays. She grabbed the candies and carefully set some of them on the tree branches. Her decorating culminated in lighting the candle she had purchased a couple of weeks before but always felt too guilty to light. The aroma of cinnamon and spice filled the air. She placed it by the tree, but not too close. *I don't want the tree to catch fire.* The candlelight flickered off the bits of foil on the candies, and Johanna felt a sense of peace she hadn't ever experienced.

It was well past midnight, and she turned her head in surprise when she heard caroling outside.

She pulled back the curtain and saw a group of people walking down the block, singing.

It's Christmas, she thought. The package she'd found on her doorstep still waited for her to unwrap it. Once again, she used her folding chair as a walker and sat on it while she picked up the parcel. She placed the package on the seat and pushed it over to the futon. She made herself comfortable before tearing off the wrapping paper. She had no idea what could be inside but knew it might be the closest she'd come to opening a gift at Christmas. Her jaw dropped when she finally cast her eyes on what was hidden inside—a first edition of *Heidi*—the same book she had been looking at in *Artiqua Literaria*. She leaned her head back against the cushion to think. The woman who owned the bookstore seemed friendly enough, but why would she give Johanna a valuable first edition? The woman didn't look poor, but she also didn't look like she made a habit out of giving books away. Johanna's heart skipped a beat when she remembered the little old man—the one who had called her 'Josefina.' *No, it can't be. How would he even know where I live?* Neither Amaranda nor Derrick had been there, nor had she told them about the book, so she felt confident it hadn't come from either of them. She opened the cover and discovered a small envelope with her name on it. Inside, a note simply said, "Merry Christmas from one book lover to another."

A single tear cascaded down her cheek.

Someone had sent her a present—a very special gift—and she knew she would treasure it as a symbol of her newfound freedom.

And maybe like Heidi—another girl orphaned at an early age—Johanna might also find her happy ending.

THE END

If you enjoyed this book, please take a moment to review it on Amazon, Goodreads, or LibraryThing. Reviews are very important to indie writers, and I would truly appreciate your effort. Thank you.

—C. A. Pack

If you want to read more about Johanna's quest for independence, turn the page for a preview of—

CHRONICLES: THE LIBRARY OF ILLUMINATION

A GUST OF cold air coming in the window made Mal shiver, but not as much as the keening that followed it. He turned in time to see the enormous beak of a flying lizard just two feet away. And then, darkness.

And so it began ...

THE TEXTURE OF the paper, the scent of the ink, the vivid contrast of dark print in relief against a creamy page — Johanna loved everything about books, reading them, touching them, owning them. She found illuminated manuscripts and finely bound texts intoxicating, and she appreciated the beauty of richly colored plates illustrating the books she read. Just like someone with drug or alcohol dependence, she always looked for her next fix.

She often dreamed of having her own library, a large wood-paneled room with floor-to-ceiling shelves filled with ancient dictionaries and atlases and centuries-old fiction. She envisioned the books that would populate the space: *The Iliad, The Od-*

yssey, a Gutenberg Bible, a first edition of *Through the Looking Glass*. Between the banks of shelves, natural light would stream in through tall windows. She could almost hear the crackle of flames as they devoured logs in a fireplace, adding atmosphere and warmth to the library of her dreams. She sighed when she thought about the gentle stretch she would feel in her thighs every time she climbed the circular stairs to a narrow balcony that circled the perimeter of the library's second story. That's where she would keep her old favorites by Poe, Shakespeare, and Brontë. Of course, her muscles would thank her as soon as she settled into the down-filled cushions of a leather sofa and propped her book on top of the soft cashmere pillow on her lap. It would be the perfect setting for reading one of her beloved tomes.

B-B-B-R-R-R-I-I-I-N-N-N-G-G-G!

Johanna hated the telephone and everything it represented. It rudely rang with no regard for what she was doing at that moment. The ring tone sounded brassy and irritating, and the people on the other end of the line were, for the most part, annoying and picayune. However, speaking to those callers happened to be an integral part of her job. "I'm a people person," she had blathered to the man who was about to become her employer. He hired her specifically to deal with clients, and all day long an unending stream of customers called, each one demanding her time and attention, with no thought that perhaps Johanna deserved the same courtesy from them.

When she first took the job at Book Services, she had high hopes about working with precious manuscripts all day, researching ancient texts, or perhaps learning bookbinding and repair. But she quickly found out the only book involved in her job contained the work orders she filled out as the calls came in. She was just another worker bee in a hive filled with countless drones.

"Where's my delivery?" "You sent the wrong books." "I don't want this anymore. Come back and get it." Demanding. Obnoxious. Exhausting. At the end of each day, she dragged herself home, bone tired and too weary to do anything except eat dinner and fall into bed with a book. Always with a book. That's when her life began, for only when she immersed herself in the pages of a well-written story did Johanna feel like life was worth living. No wonder. She'd had a tough childhood—orphaned when she could barely walk and brought up in an institution best described as utilitarian, which brooked no signs of independent thinking. Books were her only means of escape.

Johanna had grown into a curious and imaginative child, forced to bury all indications of innate intelligence if she wanted to avoid punishment and humiliation. And being preternaturally intuitive, she quickly learned to conform.

ONE FRIDAY EVENING, at the end of a particularly trying day, her boss waited until after she punched out on the time clock to tell her to pick up a package and deliver it to Mr. Henry Morton at Bay House in Exeter. "It's an emergency."

She had never heard of Mr. Morton, nor did she feel inclined to go out of her way on her own time on a rainy Friday evening to deliver a package to him. But jobs were scarce, and she needed to keep hers if she wanted to keep a roof over her head, even if the roof leaked and urgently needed to be repaired. She silently cursed but audibly agreed, and trudged out to her car.

She had trouble finding the address where Mr. Morton's package awaited her. That part of town had an abundance of winding lanes and gloomy buildings that were not clearly marked. When she finally pulled up to the structure that she *believed* matched the address her boss had given her—for the building had no number—she was surprised to find an old library she never knew existed. The name carved in the limestone lintel had nearly worn away:

The Library of Illumination

Johanna remained in her car for several minutes, listening to raindrops drum against the roof. The Library of Illumination looked closed, but she was already there, so she might as well see if anyone was inside. She ran to the building and pushed against the narrow double doors. They opened into a drab vestibule with a scarred wooden floor and dark patterned wallpaper. A small overhead fixture emitted just enough light to enable Johanna to see a worn brass plaque with narrow gills fastened to the far wall. A button that looked like a doorbell had the words *What do you seek?* engraved beneath it.

She pushed the button, but didn't hear it ring. *Just my luck,* she thought. She waited a minute and then pressed it a second time. She was again greeted by silence.

She thought about leaving and telling her boss no one had been there. She looked out the door. The rain had turned to hail, and she could hear it pitting the outside of the glass.

Annoyed, she pushed the button again, and when nothing happened, she started poking it over and over again, tears of frustration stinging her eyes. She was supposed to be home, not here wasting her time in a strange place in this dark, depressing warren of a neighborhood, just so her boss could curry favor with a client.

"YOU — CALL — THIS — ILLUMINA-TION?" she shouted, violently stabbing the button to emphasize each word.

Suddenly, the wall sprang open, and she stared into the room of her dreams. Books lined polished wooden shelves that soared overhead for several stories — so high, in fact, that the shelves actually looked like they got lost in the clouds. But of course that was impossible. She chalked it up to her need for food.

Johanna leaned her umbrella against the wall. Rivulets of water streamed down the nylon fabric and across the floor. Like a caravan of parched men lost in the desert, the old, dry floorboards welcomed the moisture, absorbing it immediately. She brushed droplets of rain from her sleeves before entering the library.

Inside, what she saw mesmerized her. The aged glass in the windows looked wavy and translucent, and although she knew a storm raged outside, these windows admitted a warm glow. Flames danced among the logs inside a two-story fireplace, and as the heat embraced her, she could smell the aroma of pine and cedar.

"Hello?" she called out.

When nobody answered, she wandered over to a large refectory table that stood off to one side. It was covered with some of the most beautiful books Johanna had ever seen. Forgetting why she was there, she inspected a thick volume on astronomy. The leather cover had a fine patina, and she carefully turned the delicate parchment pages, until the beauty of a richly colored plate illustrating the solar system arrested her attention. It was so finely detailed, she felt like she could hop right into it and glide through space. She stroked the picture with her fingers, feeling the silky smoothness of the page, but froze when a three-dimensional image appeared in midair, right in front of her. Each brightly colored planet rotated on its axis as it circled around the sun. She studied

Earth and swore she could see the storm clouds now pelting Exeter with hail.

Johanna closed the book, and the solar system disappeared. Intrigued, she gingerly walked around the room until she spotted a faded, green linen book with the words *Noah's Ark* embossed in gold on the cover. She opened it to the page recounting the animals that had boarded the ark. Her head snapped up when the roar of an elephant assailed her. There it stood—one of a pair—with its trunk held high, right in the middle of the library. She watched as a goat meandered out from behind the pachyderm, picked up a first edition of *Moby-Dick*, and started devouring it.

"Oh no!" she screamed, as she slammed the book shut. The animals disappeared, and the half-eaten Herman Melville novel dropped to the floor.

Johanna felt beads of sweat forming on her upper lip. She always perspired when scared or nervous. If she had learned anything from her childhood experiences, it was that the damaged book could mean big trouble. For her. She picked up the book and looked for an inconspicuous place to put it. Stashing it behind the leather sofa seemed like a good idea; however, she wasn't expecting what she found there. In a heap on the floor lay a scrawny little man, whose nearly bald head was punctuated by only three tufts of fluffy, white hair. He sported a pair of broken wire-rimmed spectacles that had been taped back together, and wore baggy corduroy pants and a threadbare cardigan sweater that had a tiny pin attached to it, identifying him as *Malcolm Trees, Curator*. She put her face close to the man's nose and mouth to check if he was still breathing.

"You're stealing my air."

Her heart nearly stopped. "You're alive, then?"

"Just barely. I really don't have a choice. I must remain here to watch over these books."

Johanna got down to business. "I'm here to pick up a package for Mr. Morton."

"Yes, of course," the old man replied. "If you'll do me the favor of helping me off the floor."

"What happened to you? Did you fall?"

"No. I was cranking the window shut when a wind gust lifted the cover of a book on paleontology. A pterosaur flew out and knocked me over."

He ignored her shocked expression as he continued. "Thank goodness I held on to the window crank. As I went down, I pulled the window closed. The book cover dropped back into place and that stopped the pterosaur in its tracks, or there would have been a mess in here. We're lucky it was an Istiodactylus and not one of its larger brethren, or I dare say, things might have ended differently, and you may have been attacked as soon as you entered the door."

"I wouldn't have liked that," she responded. "May I have Mr. Morton's book now?"

"Yes, yes, of course, just be careful with it.

It would never do to have gangs of Bengal tribesmen running all around Exeter, looking for witches to kill."

Johanna must have gaped at the man, because he quickly added, "Don't worry. The book is securely wrapped in brown paper and all tied up with twine in a nice, neat package. You should be perfectly safe."

She reluctantly took the package, and found her way back to the vestibule. The door slammed shut behind her, and once again, the world grew dreary. She looked around for her umbrella, but it was gone. *Great.*

She made a mad dash for her car, and carefully navigated the roads of Exeter, looking for Bay House. When she finally found it, she realized she would have to run for the door with the book stashed under her coat to protect it.

Johanna hurried, even though the walkway was slick. She hoped she wouldn't slip and fall and somehow give free rein to the fury of the men in the book she carried.

She banged the door knocker several times. *Manners be damned.* She just wanted to deliver the book and go home.

A large, muscular man pulled the door open.

"Mr. Morton?"

"You have the book?"

"Yes, I do. And it put me through quite a bit of trouble." She pulled the book from under her coat and fussed with the string that bound it.

The man pulled the book from her hands and slammed the door in her face.

"Hey," she screamed, banging the knocker. "I want a receipt for that, and I'm not leaving until I get one." But she waited in vain. In the rain. And when a bolt of lightning cracked overhead, she retreated to her car and slowly made her way home.

JOHANNA ARRIVED AT Book Services the following morning to find the pile of work on her desk had more than doubled in size. She glared at her colleague Lucinda. She felt sure the older girl worked late for the sole purpose of dumping unwanted work on Johanna's desk. Lucinda appeared to be as busy as ever and didn't looked up.

B-B-B-R-R-R-I-I-I-N-N-N-G-G-G!

Johanna closed her eyes, just for a moment, and wished she were somewhere else. The phone continued to ring until she reluctantly picked it up.

"I want to see you in my office."

Disgusted, Johanna threw her purse under her desk. *I'm only two minutes late,* she thought, and she'd spent more than an hour of her own time the previous evening making a delivery for her boss. *What does he want from me, blood?*

When she got to his cramped cubicle, he motioned for her to sit down. "How did everything go last night?"

"Fine. I got the package and delivered it to Mr. Morton, who, I might add, refused to give me a receipt for it. He just slammed the door in my face and left me standing there in the rain."

Her boss reached behind him and pulled out her umbrella. "Here. I believe you left this behind."

"I didn't leave it behind. I leaned it against the wall so it wouldn't drip water everywhere, and when I left, it wasn't there. Were you following me?"

"No. And I'm not interested in the history of your umbrella. I just want to know what you saw when you went to the ... uh ... library."

"What do you mean, what I saw?" Visions of a half-eaten *Moby-Dick* flashed before her. Had the little old man complained about her?

"Well, leaving your umbrella behind would imply that you were either there for some length of time or left in a hurry because of some atrocity."

She wouldn't really call the goat an atrocity, and she hadn't actually seen the pterosaur. However, she had been there more than a few minutes, soaking in the wonders of her dream library and the enchanted books it held.

"It took me a while to get in, you know. I think the bell is broken."

"I've never gotten in," he replied offhandedly. "Every time I turn to leave, I hear a rush of air behind me. By the time I turn back, the parcel is sitting on the floor, waiting for me. It's the oddest library I've ever been to. How can anyone look for a book there?"

Johanna broke out in goose bumps; not just a

minor plumping of her hair follicles, but major zit-sized goose mountains. *He's never been inside.*

Her boss warily eyed the tiny elevations on her skin. "Are you all right?"

She rubbed her arms with an exaggerated motion. "It's all this rain we've been having. It chills me to the core. And standing outside Mr. Morton's house waiting for a receipt didn't help. I may be coming down with something."

"I'm sure if you work your way through it, you'll be just fine. Pros play hurt, Johanna. Don't you forget that." He shooed her out of his office.

She knew he would react that way. God forbid anyone might need to take off a day from work; that simply was not allowed. They were given one week of vacation a year, and employees who took sick days received no pay. They were each forced to sign an agreement accepting those conditions before they were hired.

A WEEK LATER, her boss again waited until the last minute to ask Johanna to pick up a book and deliver it to the priory in Exeter.

Why does it have to be Exeter again? Why can't it be a little closer? At least it wasn't raining. She left work and steered her way to the library. She thought she'd find it more easily, considering she'd been there before, but if she didn't know better, she would think it had changed locations. She drove up and down the winding streets for several minutes before she finally found it.

Inside, the vestibule remained unchanged. She pressed the button, straining to listen for a ringing sound. Again, nothing happened. She thought back to her previous visit and what she had said and done. She remembered punching the bell, but couldn't remember what she said. She focused on the small brass plaque. *What are you seeking?*

She pressed the button a second time and said, "I'm here to pick up a book for the priory." Nothing happened. She pressed it again. "I'm seeking entrance." Still nothing.

"Open sesame." "Let me in." "Why are you doing this to me?" "Is this thing broken?" With each request, her voice grew louder and her actions more animated. Disillusioned, she leaned her forehead against the button. "How can you call this a Library of Illumination when no one will illuminate me on how to get in?"

The wall slid open, revealing the splendor she remembered from the previous week.

She stepped inside. The little old man was nowhere to be found. She peeked behind the couch. He wasn't there. Neither was the book the goat had snacked on during her previous visit.

She perused the titles of books scattered about the area until her eyes came to rest on *Little Women*. She had first read it at the age of thirteen, and loved the Louisa May Alcott book so much, she often daydreamed about being Jo. She opened it to a random page and read to herself.

Suddenly, Jo sat before her in a barber chair, arguing with a man over how much he should pay her for her hair. "Twenty-five dollars and not a penny less," she demanded.

Johanna watched in amazement as the barber picked up a strand of Jo's long, luxurious hair and fingered it. "All right. But don't let this get around, or you'll send me to the poorhouse." He combed her hair back from her face and tied it with a string. Picking up a pair of shears, he cut off her ponytail and gently placed the locks on a counter. He then snipped Jo's hair shorter and shorter, until he'd littered the floor with her severed tresses.

"Oh, dear."

Johanna slammed the book shut and whirled around to find the little old man staring at the floor. "I ... I ... I came to pick up a book for the priory," she stammered.

"I have it right here. But I must ask you to linger a moment and help me out. My lumbago is acting up." He shuffled across the room and opened a narrow closet hidden in the wall paneling. "In here. There's a shovel and a broom. Would you please sweep up those hair clippings? I wouldn't want to slip and fall."

Johanna took the broom and shovel and returned to where she had seen Jo getting a haircut. Jo may have vanished, but bits of her hair lay all over the floor.

A foul odor emanated from the broom as Johanna swept. She wrinkled her nose.

The little old man apparently noticed. "That broom still stinks, does it? I tried cleaning it, but I guess I didn't do a good job. I must need new spectacles. But it's your own fault, you know. Those animals from *Noah's Ark* left quite a mess last week, and I believe that was all your doing."

Noah's Ark? Johanna thought about the elephants and other animals. She had been so busy trying to get the book away from the goat that she hadn't given much thought to what the other animals may have left behind.

"What should I do with this?" She jiggled the shovel containing the pile of loose hair.

The little old man pulled on a handle near the closet door. It opened up into a chute. "In here," he answered.

Johanna dumped the snippets, and Malcolm Trees nodded toward the closet. She put the tools away without saying another word.

He picked up a parcel and handed it to her. "Be careful. Templars can be ruthless."

She nodded, and delivered the package as instructed.

THE FOLLOWING MORNING, Johanna found a huge pile of work on her desk, no doubt due to another nocturnal visit from lazy Lucinda. She busied herself with getting it done, so she wouldn't have to stay late.

Johanna's boss startled her. "How did it go last night?" He had actually come out to her desk to ask about the book delivery, rather than call her into his office. Even Lucinda stopped typing and gawked at him.

"Fine," Johanna answered, not offering him any additional information.

He stared at her in silence for a minute or so, then walked away without saying another word.

"What's that all about?" Lucinda asked casually.

"I have no idea," Johanna answered. "Why don't you ask him?"

Lucinda returned to her typing, with a scowl on her face. About the only things she and Johanna had in common were that they worked for the same company and neither of them liked their boss. He reminded Johanna of the cold and calculating headmaster who had used an iron fist to rule the orphanage in which she grew up. She didn't know why Lucinda hated their boss, but she knew Lucinda would never ask him *anything*.

A FEW DAYS LATER, Johanna's boss told her she would have to pick up two parcels and deliver them to two different destinations.

She didn't mind visiting the library, but she hated her boss for intruding on her personal time. She thought he waited until the last minute to ask her to make deliveries as a demonstration of *his* power over *her* job. She wondered if he told her to make two deliveries because he had tried to make one himself and had failed.

"Where are they going?"

"They'll give you the addresses at the library."

"I hope they're local," she said, walking toward the door. "I don't have a lot of gasoline to devote to running all over creation. And my fuel costs are getting out of hand. I asked the garage to send you the bill."

She watched his face turn white, then red, just before the door closed behind her. She hadn't really asked anyone to send him the bill, but saying so made her feel like she was taking back control of her life. She smiled. She didn't do it often, but when she did her face instantly changed, and her beauty emerged.

IN EXETER, SHE again felt like someone had switched the streets around. It took her an extra half-hour to find the library, and it seemed like she stumbled upon it by accident.

She entered the vestibule and walked over to the button on the brass plaque. She pressed it and said, "Illumination." The doors opened, and she walked inside, smiling at having figured out the key to gaining entrance.

The little old man stood waiting for her. "Feeling pretty proud of yourself, are you?"

"What do you mean?"

"Very few people come to our door, and rarely does anyone gain admittance. It would seem that hardly anyone ever seeks illumination. They punch the button, pound on the door, and rant and rave in general, but no one is going to get in unless they say the right thing.

"You managed to gain entrance the first couple of times through sheer, dumb luck."

He said it matter-of-factly and without malice, but Johanna's smile vanished. Her mind immediately transported back in time to the orphanage in which each child had been treated with such contempt, they couldn't help but feel worthless.

The headmaster of the orphanage had been invited to sit in on the youngsters' weekly spelling lesson. Their teacher made a big fuss over him, and he began drilling the students.

Johanna waited her turn with both enthusiasm and trepidation. She wanted to excel, but she feared humiliation.

"Johanna, spell judgment.*"*

Johanna stood ramrod straight, her excitement building. Her teacher had just gone over the spelling the previous day, and Johanna had memorized it. She really wanted to impress the headmaster, and she now had a chance to shine.

"Judgment, j-u-d-g-m-e-n-t, judgment."

Her teacher nodded his head in approval until the headmaster shouted out, "Wrong!"

Her teacher just stared, his mouth hanging open.

"There is an E *in* judgment. *J-u-d-g-e-m-e-n-t."*

Johanna knew she was right. She spelled it just the way she had been taught, and she stood her ground. "I spelled it correctly," she stated, with a slight quiver.

"You dare to challenge me?" the headmaster bellowed. "Prepare to be punished severely."

Johanna looked to her teacher for support, but found none.

The headmaster left the room momentarily, and returned carrying a massive Oxford English Dictionary *and a cat-o'-nine-tails. He scanned the well-worn dictionary to letters beginning with* J, *and there it was: j-u-d-g-e-m-e-n-t. It didn't matter that the OED also included the other spelling; only that Johanna be punished for defying him.*

He whipped Johanna five times in front of her classmates. Her teacher had betrayed her by not defending her. Her so-called friends made fun of her afterwards. As a result, Johanna learned to embrace isolation and numb her feelings against pain.

"What impressed me," Malcolm Trees continued, "is how you learned from it."

But Johanna didn't hear his last sentence. She had already switched to self-preservation mode. She masked her feelings of inadequacy with a harsh retort. "Why don't you just give me the parcels then, and we'll be done with it."

"Wait here," he answered, surprised at her sudden change of mood. Her curt manner made him involuntarily retaliate. "And for heaven's sake, don't open any books."

"Be quick about it, then. I haven't got all night." Her own rudeness shocked her, but she would rather die than let this little old man know he had the power to hurt her.

The first parcel was very large. "You'd better hold this with both hands. It's an encyclopedia, and lord knows what page it might open up to if you should drop it. You could unleash the tidal waves caused by the sinking of Atlantis, the hideous and painful boils from the bubonic plague, or perhaps the bombing of Hiroshima. It could be catastrophic."

"Where's it going?"

"Look here," he said, thumping the top of the package. "It's practically around the corner."

"Is there a second package?"

"Oh. Yes. I have it right here." He walked over to the desk and took a miniature parcel out of the drawer. "I'll slip this into your pocket," he said, matching word to deed. "You had best deliver the larger one first."

The encyclopedia weighed a ton, and Johanna rested it on the refectory table to get a better grip. In doing so, she knocked Charles Dickens' *A Christmas Carol* on the floor, and the Ghost of Christmas Past sprang into action, conjuring up a festive ball. In an instant, Mr. and Mrs. Fezziwig danced around the library, swirling to and fro, knocking more books onto the floor. Suddenly, a young boy in a wheelchair began asking where he could find *The Secret Garden*. Trying to avoid him, the Fezziwigs danced right into a British soldier, who held the body of *Gunga Din*. They all went down hard, causing mass confusion.

"Go," the little old man said, pushing Johanna toward the door. "I'll deal with this."

Johanna suddenly found herself alone in the dim vestibule, clutching the encyclopedia for dear life. She didn't remember actually walking out the door. She felt almost as if the old man had transported her there by magic.

She carefully placed the large parcel on the seat of her car, and drove to the address written on it. The old man had been right about the location. She probably could have walked there if she weren't afraid of dropping the encyclopedia and unleashing who knows what.

After the first delivery, she took out the smaller package and looked at the address. Her stomach lurched when she saw *her* name and address on it. She slipped it back into her pocket and drove home. She wanted to make sure she was someplace safe and familiar before opening it.

Johanna's attached cottage could almost be called ramshackle, even though she worked hard every weekend to keep it from deteriorating. She had a small living room, a smaller bedroom, a tiny kitchen, and a minuscule bathroom—pleasant but humble. It wasn't her dream home, but it was all she could afford. She was only seventeen years old, and she liked being able to say she lived in a one-bedroom flat, even though she had friends with studio apartments larger than all her rooms added together. Now it looked like she would lose her home to a developer who wanted to build condominiums. Her landlord had informed her she would have to move out by the end of the year. *Perhaps my next flat will let me have a cat,* she mused. At least one positive thing might result from her dilemma.

She locked the door and pulled down the shades before taking out the tiny parcel. It would never do to have a neighbor witness something that might be difficult to explain.

She sat on the diminutive sofa in her living room and gingerly opened the package. Inside, she found a small journal. It had the initials *J.C.* stamped on the front cover. *My initials.* How did the man at the library know her name?

She began to lift the cover but stopped suddenly, breaking into a cold sweat. *What if J.C. stands for Jesus Christ and they start crucifying him here in my living room?* She imagined the crowd roaring for blood. She could practically see the dust rising as Christ dragged the cross to the field of execution. She smelled the sweat of the Roman soldiers leading the way. *Or is that me?*

She didn't know what to do. She thought back to her early years in school, when her teachers forced her to sit through Bible instruction. She had daydreamed through a lot of it, but was pretty sure no one had ever mentioned Jesus Christ keeping a diary. She had to chance it; after all, her address must have been written on the package for a reason.

She opened the cover. The fly page had been dedicated to her:

> *To Johanna Charette,*
> *You seek Illumination.*
> *May these pages embrace your imagination and feed your soul.*
> *Regards,*
> *Malcolm Trees, Curator*
> *The Library of Illumination*

Malcolm Trees? The little old man in the library had given her a gift. She felt awful about having been rude to him. Maybe she should bake him some brownies to smooth things over. *Does he even have any teeth?* She made up her mind. She would

bake light, fluffy muffins. She wouldn't add nuts.
Carefully, she turned to the first diary page.
It had that day's date on it. She removed a tiny pen
from a loop attached to the book. Then carefully,
very carefully, she wrote about the day's events.
As she wrote, she nervously looked up from
time to time, expecting to see her words come alive.
But every word she wrote stayed firmly on the page.
When she finished, she locked the diary with a tiny
key that had been tied to its blue ribbon bookmark
and slipped the key into her purse. She hid the diary in the back of a cupboard, behind her supply of
bathroom tissue. *It should be safe here.*

Visit my website at www.carolpack.com

CHRONICLES: THE LIBRARY OF ILLUMINATION

SECOND CHRONICLES OF ILLUMINATION

Available on Amazon.com

About the Author

C. A. Pack is the author of the YA supernatural series *Library of Illumination/Chronicles of Illumination*, as well as the historical fiction, *Code Name: Evangeline*, and the fantasy, *Evangeline's Ghost*. She is an award-winning former journalist and television news anchor, working in the New York metropolitan area.The author is a member of International ThrillerWriters, and Sisters in Crime, and has formerly served as president of the Press Club of Long Island. She lives in Westbury, NY, with her husband, a couple of picky parrots, and dozens of imaginary characters who constantly demand page space.